claire

Copyright

Cover design by Jacqueline & Jane Lau

Part 1: Monsters & Pirates

Small

"A person is an Island," the Therapist began.

"A person is what?" Patient Seven snarled, their pupils dilating with a mixture of rage and fear.

"An Island. A person is an Island," the Therapist repeated. Her soft, soothing voice was affected by the sense of dread often felt when meeting Patient Seven for the first time. "Use this thinking to guide your healing," she continued, her speech becoming shakier with every moment that the Patient refused to blink when staring directly into her eyes.

"I thought I had escaped all this," Patient Seven sighed.

"Please, I need you to comply. Um, what was your name again?"

"Which one, and what does it matter? No more names, no more islands. Please leave me alone. I just need a bath, and I will be fine again," Patient Seven interjected.

"Oh, right, your name is 'Aqua...'? You're the one who loves water?" the Therapist piped up, knowing exactly when to change the subject. "And, would you describe yourself as male or female?"

"I am both, but also neither. My preferred pronouns are 'they' and 'them'," Patient Seven clarified.

"OK," the Therapist nodded, making a mental note of that. "Maybe you could tell me why you feel more comfortable in water than anywhere else?"

"Why?"

"Oh, because we.../ want to help you. But first I will need more information."

"OK," Patient Seven nodded, inhaling deeply to gather their strength. "I will tell you my story. I am not an island, but I am who I am because of one. I thought that I had escaped it, but somehow it always finds me. At the start, I had a different name – I was a very peculiar thing. I was not myself; I was...

"Small. The creature named 'Small' began life as a tiny, flesh-pink tadpole. They were born from a soft, gelatinous egg that clung and camouflaged with reeds at the bottom of a small stream. After a short while of erratic swimming, gorging on algae, and avoiding the mouths of predators, Small grew four tiny legs with rounded blobs for feet with which they used to crawl out of the water towards a dark, damp cave.

Their tail became absorbed into their body whilst their back legs began to elongate. Instead of walking on all fours, they found they could stride with their two legs whilst their forelimbs developed into arms and rather stubby but still useful hands. During these physical changes, they stayed hidden in their cave. They were so soft, vulnerable, and afraid of the world around them.

Then one day, Small found the courage to emerge from their cave and meet the colours of a beautiful rainforest. Their eyes were overwhelmed by a vivid rainbow of floral pigments, a network of birdsong and a paradise of perfume. Fresh fruit was in abundance, and a calming, circulating breeze invigorated the surroundings. However, the Island was by far from perfect, as Small soon found out.

First, there was a crippling cold. Now, Small could be at best described as a tender, thin-skinned, blob-like creature. Terrified of the temperature drop and the hiss of icy winds, Small would hide in the perceived safety of their cave. They warmed themselves with the flames of a small fire they had managed to create from gathering dry twigs and small stones.

However, violent storms brought floods to the forests and flushed out Small from their cave. There was no choice but to learn how to swim up to the higher ground. Whilst water engulfed most of the Island, Small used tree branches as temporary resting points. Tired of shivering, Small had to develop thickened, blubbery skin to survive the sudden glacial harshness.

Small caught a sudden wave and let it carry them to the majestic rocks of the hill at the highest point of the Island. Scrabbling up stony paths, Small found another cave at a higher altitude. They thanked their thickened skin with its new turquoise hue and the thick, matted green hair that had sprouted from their head, for protection against the unforgiving gusts. They had also developed an increased lung capacity to adapt to the Island's summit.

As they waited for the floods to recede, they amused themselves by studying the mysterious artwork that decorated the walls of the hilltop caves. Indistinguishable symbols, pictures of animals and depictions of the sun and the moon entertained Small for a long while."

"So, despite the harsh weather conditions, you had a tropical Island of adventure all to yourself?" the Therapist interrupted. "Lucky you."

"Not me, I'm talking about Small. *Small* had a tropical Island," Patient Seven stated forcefully. "Small!"

"OK, Small did," the Therapist backed down. "Lucky them."

"Small certainly felt lucky. After every hardship, they became anything they needed to be to survive the challenges of their Island," Patient Seven carried on.

"When the hilltops moved and shook due to earthquakes, they sent stones ricocheting off the cliffs that almost fell on Small as they slept. It meant that Small then developed the ability to sense murmurs of the earth before the rocks crushed them. When the hilltops jolted, and almost kicked them back down into the flooded forests, Small learned to swim up and out of the murky waters and climb their way back to safety. Small evolved into a being of little-to-no sleep. They stayed alert no matter how exhausted they were.

As the floodwater retreated to the ocean, Small expanded their 'map' of the Island that they had created on the floor of their cave using stones, twigs, and charred wood from recently made fires. They used their newfound 'artistic' ability to 'collect' the sights of the unpredictable Island that they called home. Stones from every new-found region of the Island were gathered and organised to give Small a tactile awareness of a world that could change at any moment."

"Yes, I see that you still collect stones," the Therapist noticed.

"Yes, stones, shells, seeds, nuts. You never know when you might need food or if you want to give someone a gift," Patient Seven elaborated as they reached towards pebbles decorating the windowsill of their room. "Perhaps I will give you a gift."

"Oh...I'm not allowed to take gifts from Patients," the Therapist cut in, raising her palms defensively.

"I am not a Patient," Patient Seven stated with a deadly serious tone. "Anyway..."

"So, climbing and re-climbing up the rocks as well as swimming so much surely made you strong? Do you like being strong?" the Therapist interrupted.

"Climbing rocks was the beginning. Small had to be strong to fight a demon that lurked in every nook and cranny of that Island. I call this 'The Grip'.

"When Small journeyed back into the forests to search for food, they had to battle tree roots, vines and sometimes sinking sand. Everything about the Island would try to hold them and restrict their movement. It seemed like in every direction; there was a trap waiting for Small. They had no choice but to develop stronger muscles and endurance so that they could pull themselves out from the sinking sand or struggle against the suffocating vines.

Cool, soothing waterfalls and rivers provided some relief from the asphyxiating presence that had cursed Small's Island home. When Small paddled in rivers and floated on logs, they felt a strange safety and an affinity for the movement of the river water. Perhaps it reminded them of their younger days as a tadpole. The river flow jostled and wound around any obstacle and the tiny fish inhabiting it went about their lives, responding to the flow of the water, just as Small had done. The river gave Small a sense of peace and calm for the first time in a long time.

One day, Small climbed aboard a fallen log and used it to follow the river as it flowed downhill through The Grip of the forests. They escaped weeping willows and their tangling drapes and swerved to avoid dangerous falling branches that would have seriously hurt them if Small had not been agile enough.

The land became steeper, and rapids almost jolted Small from their wooden float. To keep from being separated, Small's hands and feet grew sharp claws that could dig into the damp fibres of the log.

Rapids gave way to a sharp cliff edge and the blood-curdling height of an upcoming waterfall. Small grinned and bared it as they plummeted with the river flow, down to a crystalline bowl of water below. Both exhilarated by the refreshing catch of the pool and exhausted; they let go of their wooden log and let themselves be carried down the river out to sea.

Realising that they were able to hold their breath for minutes at a time and open their eyes underwater without much discomfort, they swam beside shoals of salmon and bass travelling with the river flow. Small's hands and feet started to shape themselves into webbed claws as the river became broader and deeper. By the time the river had met the sea, Small's body had grown longer, and their skin had become more scaly, with a colour that had transformed from a pale turquoise into one with blue-green stripes that enabled camouflage with their environment.

Happy to have developed large, webbed feet, they torpedoed through the realm of the underwater. Small passed through luscious reefs, brimming with clouds of shoaling fish. Octopuses gazed with intrigue as Small swam past. They had found a paradise, but Small was not fully able to appreciate this new world – at least not yet.

Storm clouds approached, and Small felt the sea become more turbulent. They whooshed through the ocean towards a rocky outcrop separated from the Island's stony beach by a moat of unpredictable waves. A voice sang through the whistling wind as Small sat cross-legged on their rock.

"You've almost left the Island, so I see. Surely, you will feel better if you return to me?" the air swooned, deploying a woozy tune.

"But it's you who has pushed me out to sea!" Small yelled back assertively, feeling their voice becoming louder with every word. "After the storm, who knows what I'll be?"

So there, Small sat, surrounded by the crashing waves and chaotic breeze, staring back at the Island through their opal-blue eyes. As the sea smashed against the rock, Small sighed and found their calm and replied to the Island,

"I have been preparing for this since I was born, to weather the weather. For this is my storm…"

The Listener

"This all sounds incredibly dangerous," the Therapist interjected.

"You say this now? After everything I've told you?" Patient Seven grumbled.

"I mean, most people would not have survived anything you've spoken about," the Therapist replied quickly, trying her best to suppress signs of disbelief. "Can you confirm for me one thing – do you think that you are a person, or would you refer to yourself as something else?"

"Thank you for even thinking of it," Patient Seven smiled bashfully. "I have tried many times to be a person in the way that you probably think of the word. I am more creature, or monster, to be quite honest with you. I am whatever I need to be, and I am whatever you want to see in me. Just call me a creature if you want to keep things simple."

"And on that Island, on that rock, you, or Small, needed to be...something. Is it what Small *wanted* to be, though?"

"What Small *wanted* was never important," Patient Seven sighed. "At the time, probably yes. Any way that Small could beat the terrors of that Island or survive the loneliness of that rock, Small let whatever needed to happen, happen. What Small *wanted* – that is a separate thing."

"How did you keep so calm when you sat on that rock?"

"Don't you dare laugh if I tell you," Patient Seven frowned.

"I would never do that," the Therapist added quickly.

"If you laugh, I will flood the room," Patient Seven threatened.

"I would never laugh at you," the Therapist reinforced sternly, sitting more upright than before.

"Small... sang to themselves. As the sky roared, as the wind pushed into them and as the waves tried to pull, crush, or engulf them, Small clung to the rock with their strong claws. They serenaded the sea with vocal cords that became more powerful with every word they sang. With every chant, the calmer they felt and the more they became connected to the ocean. As if it had 'heard' their song, the sea became calmer near to Small's rock. The water swirled around where Small sat, leaving them to sing in peace.

After the storm, the waves patted the beach gently; the clouds drifted to reveal a cerulean sky and the sea soothingly sloshed against Small's rock."

"Did you return to the Island?" asked the Therapist.

"*Small* did not. Well, not immediately. Although they craved the jungle fruits, the freshwater of the rivers and the shelter of the caves, they made do with what they could find when the tide receded. The retreating ocean left behind pristine rock pools with an abundance of shellfish, anemones, and seaweed for Small to gorge on. They ate a lot, and often became lost in the comfort of easy food. They had quickly learned how to grab small fish from the rockpools, either to feast on or to use as bait to lure larger creatures. Their teeth became sharper and jagged to crunch through the shells of crabs and shrimp.

Coconuts and their succulent milk fulfilled Small's thirst and provided bowls with which to collect the shellfish for meals later. However, the more time Small spent on the Island, especially near the forests, the more they understood that it was not their home. They did not feel the comfort that they felt surrounded by the sea."

"Too many memories?" the Therapist asked.

"Yes, but also, there were the screams," Patient Seven expressed intensely. "In the air that travelled through the Island and circled back to the sea – Small could hear cries of suffering and sadness. Often, they had to go back to the sea and dive into the water to fill their ears with anything else except the sounds of that mysterious horror. If Small were too tired to swim, they would float head-up in the water but with their ears submerged, and they would gaze up at the clouds and blue sky, or up at the artwork of the night's star-scapes. Either way, they would self-soothe by singing to themselves.

When the water was rough, Small begged it to take them away from the Island. However dangerous the journey would be, they would adapt to cope with whatever peril. Small's mind filled with thousands of thoughts about how they would leave the Island, but there was something still chaining them to it. There was something about the Island they needed to understand before they left it. Amidst the screeching winds, the Island would sing;

"Come back, Small thing; you must miss your cave. You want to escape, but you are not so brave. The Island still has more to teach you. Let it tell you what is real, what is true. You belong here, not the ocean blue."

Small would repeatedly dive to escape the songs, evolving an ability to hold their breath for longer and longer times. Their neck burst into a dashboard of gills that enabled Small to breathe underwater and with each breath, feel less suffocated by the Island's influence. There was the urge to swim far away from the Island whilst

Small was underwater, but adapting to every nuance of the sea exhausted as much as elated them.

Whilst sitting cross-legged under the sea, surrounded by a utopia of kaleidoscopic reefs, Small grabbed the attention of a hunting party of ravenous sharks. As a defence mechanism, Small's back erupted to produce a collection of sharp, cartilaginous spikes to ward off predators. Despite evolving so much and so quickly, Small had not developed the ability to evade exhaustion. The tiredness hit them so abruptly that they had to climb back onto their rock and collapse for a while.

Amidst the screams and songs from the Island – a constant push-pull effect on Small's psyche that they attempted to fight with their weary vocals, they heard a very different type of music. It was refreshing, uplifting – even life-giving! Small slid back into the water and swam towards the beauteous harmonies as they permeated through the ocean. Their ears led them to a large, white, floating object that was attached to the seabed with a strong rope and metal anchor.

Cautiously, Small surfaced and examined the floating curiosity. They saw that one edge of the boat presented a little ladder with which they clambered up. Clumsily slipping onto the wooden deck, they attempted to figure out the origin of the music. The boat itself was a white cabin-cruiser with elegant edges painted navy blue. It had possibly seen better days and most definitely needed re-painting in some places.

On the deck, there were signs that life had been there. Open packets of tasty, salty food littered the boat. There was a small net with a measly catch of bait, a pile of citrus fruits and a barrel of what seemed to be river water. Further along, there was one huge, slightly soggy cardboard box containing an impressive collection of vinyl records.

At the helm of the boat, there were no apparent controls or steering wheel. Instead, there was a wooden vinyl record player that seemed to play music by itself. There was no one else there, yet.

"Hello there! Who lives here?" Small slurred, noticing how clumsy their words were after talking to nobody but themselves or the Island for what seemed like many lifetimes.

Small did find the owner of the boat – they were floating beside their vessel, face down in the seawater. Bubbles surfaced from around their head. Small did not immediately know what to do, but instinctively, they hauled the poor drowning soul back onto the deck of their boat and laid them, face-up. He was tiny and almost as light as a twig. The record player suddenly started to play after a moment of silence and played a song eerily relevant to the situation.

"Give your new friend your air, a mouth behind his thick hair..." the lyrics beamed.

The music was correct – Small noticed that their new friend had more hair than a face. Jet black locks covered his eyes and flowed around his nose and mouth. Small placed one webbed claw onto the hairy guy's forehead and the other hand gently underneath his chin. They made sure to open the man's airway before breathing into his fuzzy mouth.

The man sat up suddenly and regurgitated seawater. The newly conscious boatman stared at Small with his piercing brown eyes partially covered by his soggy, black locks.

"Who are you?" Small asked them, choking back their initial shyness and disbelief.

The boatman smiled happily with a full set of sharp, pearl-coloured teeth. He reached into the box of records to replace the current harmony with a very different song. Bass notes, a chorus of various voices and a cheerful drumbeat filled the moment. He then showed Small the cover of the album. The picture seemed to be a vague depiction of himself with his flowing black hair, vinyl player and soggy linens that were at least one size too big for him. The writing on the cover was almost incomprehensible but helped by the lyrics in the background.

"I am the Listener, and I hear the world's wrongs. My boat is here because I heard your songs."

The record beamed sounds of waves crashing and a storm rumbling against wobbly vocals. The Listener pointed at the record and then at Small, who shrugged and extended their

24

claw to shake the furry, ticklish hand of the Listener.

"My name is…," Small began, but could not finish. They had no idea who they were. The song carried on.

"*My boat goes to where it's needed, you see. It is time to leave your Island, will you come with me? We can both follow the music, and explore the sea*?"

Small was thrilled – the sea had responded to their plight and had given them an answer in the form of a magic music boat, or something. There was only one issue. In the time that it took Small to rescue the Listener, exchange names and think about their answer, the ocean had receded and left the boat stuck on the rocky, seaweed coated shore. Small felt as though their dream had been dumped back onto their Island.

"*What's wrong with this Island? What is the story here? There's a sick air of suffering and screams are what I hear, on this small land of fear*," the music carried on until it became drowned out by the screeching winds and the call of an Island that did not want Small to leave.

"Stay here," Small ordered the Listener. "If you have to fight, here's...something," Small winced as they pulled a spike from out of their back. The Listener cautiously took it as Small gasped in pain whilst a new spine quickly grew back in its place.

Small was about to jump out of the boat when the Listener stopped them. He pointed to the other side of the cover of the vinyl album playing. The artwork was of a monstrous creature with scales and spikes, webbed, jagged claws and opal-blue eyes. The beast cried tears that cascaded down their tough, turquoise skin. From glimpsing their nightmarish reflection on the surface of the sea before, Small knew that the creature was them. That creature was me. That creature *is* me.

"*This Island will drag you down. You will feel torn and in tatters. This Island may make you feel Small, but your real name is Aqua Maddas,*" the record sang as the Listener pointed at the image and then towards me.

"Wow," I gasped, motionless at first. Energy started building in me. It erupted as I yelled out towards the Island, "Do you hear this?! Do you hear this, Island?! My name is Aqua Maddas, and you will let us leave! What on earth is it that you want from me?!"

I leapt out of the boat and looked for something I could use to make a weapon. I found a long wooden stick near to the forest and used some tough sea kelp to tie another of my back spikes onto its end to make a rudimentary spear. Armed with my spear, I ran as fast as my clumsy, long webbed feet could allow.

I hurried towards the heart of the Island, head-first, back through the Grip of the jungle. Spear-swipes and the spikes on my back cut me free from the snatching vines, and my webbed feet saved me from engulfment by sinking sand. I ran to where the Island's song was calling me – back to the caves on top of the hill.

There, the rocks had moulded themselves into an ominous figure. They were almost human-like, but twice my height. I looked up to see the black, hollow eyes of a cold Golem that I felt had been watching and controlling me ever since I was Small. I was beyond scared. The part of me that was once Small trembled and winced, but I held the confidence gained from the

Listener's recognition of me for as long as my mental strength let me.

"Welcome back, whoever you are. The sea has made you tough and tall. But you must know something. You're from this Island, and you will always be Small," growled a deep voice emanating from the rocks. "And as you will accept and come to see, this Island holds your legacy."

The ground cracked underneath my feet. I instantly fell into a dark cavern below the hilltop. My claws could not save me from such a drop as I heard the stone figure chant "...as you will come to see..."

I flung myself into a fight-ready stance after the tumble and saw that the cave had lit itself with rounded, luminescent blue lights attached to the walls. It revealed to me a gigantic cavern full of skeletons and what seemed to be an endless sea of bony remains.

"What...is...this?" I gasped, feeling suffocated by the atmosphere.

"You are the Guardian of the Island of the Fallen. Accept your role, or I will wall you in," warned the voice from above."

"So, what was this... graveyard?" the Therapist asked.

"I had asked the same thing. As the Golem said to me – 'this Island is cursed by those who have fallen, a place of sadness - a place of solemn'," Patient Seven explained.

"OK," the Therapist gasped, furiously writing in her notebook.

"The Golem told me 'the Island of the fallen was created just for me, fed from a past of suffering in which no one can flee.' But I told the rock creature that 'I needed to be free!'," Patient Seven exclaimed.

"So, I clawed my way out of that cave as rocks crumbled under my hands and feet, trying to knock me back down into the darkness. I hauled my way to the surface as tree roots tried to Grip me. I still had my spear and used it to slash myself free from the suffocating vegetation that tried to grab my limbs.

I scrambled through the jungle, exhausted but pushing myself to keep going. The voice of the Island tried its best to hypnotise me back to sleep and trap me in soft sinking sand. The music from the Listener's boat amplified through to me, energising my jungle fight. With all the energy I had left, I ran head-first through the forest. Spines erupted from my forehead to become sharp horns that I used to slash through the sentient curtains of the jungle.

As I reached the beach, the cold rain started to fall, and another storm approached.

"Wherever I am, whatever my form, I am not this Island, and this is my storm!" I yelled as I grabbed onto the Listener's boat and pushed it into the rising tide. I leapt on board and let the ocean sweep us into its welcoming chaos.

"I trust you, boatman, and I trust the sea. Do what you need to set me free!"

That was the last thing I sang to the Island as the Listener slid about the boat, trying to change the record. All I remember is the scratch of vinyl before I collapsed and gave myself up to a storm that I hoped would break me away from the Island for good. The next thing I saw when I woke up was that the Listener and I were floating in a calm sea with no land for miles."

"So, the sea provided me with an escape and gave me freedom," Patient Seven concluded. "That's why I have such an affinity for water and the ocean."

"Wow, what a story," the Therapist grinned awkwardly, jotting down some notes onto a pad of paper before closing it hurriedly. "Thank you for sharing that with me, it's been incredibly entertaining."

"I am glad," Patient Seven replied with a forced grin.

"So, just to be clear, you became Aqua Maddas because your friend, the Listener, told you that that was your name? Before that, you were named Small?" the Therapist asked.

"Small was an inferior creature. Aqua Maddas is my real self," Patient Seven clarified.

"Perhaps we could talk more about your name in one of our next sessions. What, exactly, do those words mean to you?"

"I think I am still trying to figure that out myself," Patient Seven chuckled. "Just call me Maddas to keep things simple."

"OK, Maddas," the Therapist nodded, although her disbelief was apparent.

"What's your name?" Maddas asked.

"Um…Susan," the Therapist blurted, almost regretting it instantly.

"Now Susan, are you sure you don't want a pebble?" Maddas tried once more.

"No, but you must have this medicine to help you sleep," the Therapist replied with a stern tone to her voice.

"Sure, of course, I will take it," Patient Seven grinned. They had become very adept at the pretence of compliance. "See you next time," they chirped as they waved goodbye to Susan. As soon as she had left, Maddas immediately ran to their dormitory bathroom and flushed their medicine down the toilet.

High

The shrill of an alarm sounded through the mental health ward whilst clouds above threatened to bring heavy rain. Maddas had a habit of dancing on an outdoor tennis table in the yard, mostly when rain was about to fall. As they danced, they would often make plans to use the table to help them jump onto the nearby roof to escape from the unit. Perhaps that was why they could hear the alarm. Maybe that was why the Nurses were so enthusiastic about guiding them off the table and back inside.

"A storm is best felt outside!" Patient Seven cried — beaming their chaotic energy into the communal area of the ward and attracting the attention of other patients in the vicinity. "Come out! Come dance with me! There's more to life than being safe!"

There was only so much time that Maddas could avoid sedation. An hour after swallowing something to kill their buzz, they were asked by Susan, the Therapist about why they still were so energetic.

"Storms set me free, of course!" Patient Seven enthused, waving their webbed hands to make wild gestures that seemed not to match their words entirely. "Hearing the rain – it brings me such happiness. If I can't have a bath here, I will catch the rain on my skin and breathe."

Susan sat again with Maddas in their dormitory room. Her presence calmed the patient seemingly much more than any medication could. She also seemed to calm down the people trying their best to restrain the aquatic humanoid.

"Maddas, can you tell me the first time you have felt like this?" Susan asked.

"Feel what? Be more specific. I feel everything!" Patient Seven cried.

"High," Susan defined more precisely.

"The first time was just after I had escaped from the Island," Patient Seven began. "I was finally free and surrounded by the glistening, azure water of the sea and endless hidden ocean treasures. My new home was on a magic musical boat with the company of my fantastic little fluffy friend, the Listener. He had an unlimited supply of music from every culture, every time, and every creature! I needed to explore and experience everything, and immediately!

I remember the Listener standing back, creating space between himself and me when I became too hyperactive. I recall the shocked expression that he tried to hide with his hairy face as I examined vinyl covers full of colour and pointed at every one of them. To the ones with landscapes, I would shout "We need to go there!" If there was a person, "We need to meet them!" If it was uninterpretable art, it was, "I don't understand, but I want to learn how to!"

Before the Listener could even put on any one of the records that I had singled out, I would also look to the sea and swoon that I needed to swim, I wanted to go fishing or that I must communicate with every aquatic creature.

One of the record covers showed a map of the ocean and all the islands large and small that punctuated our aquatic home. I remember the Listener quietly laughing at me as I pointed to at least fifty different locations and instructed him to take us to all of them, probably all the same time.

Freedom made me feel as high as the seabirds that swooped to catch flying fish. I felt as energetic and playful as the pods of dolphins that whistled and clicked as they jumped out of the sea to greet us. I was sizzling with electricity like the electric eels and rays that hunted the reefs below where I would explore and hunt for succulent oysters.

There were so many monsters back then. We mostly stayed out of each other's way, but it did not stop me from admiring the majestic, long-necked, underwater beasts such as the Styxosaurus and the Mauisarus as they hunted in the deep. I would gaze, wide-eyed at the Megalodon sharks, larger than the human buses of today. I would respect and be inspired by gigantic stingrays that would block out light from the sun as I dived underneath them.

There were times when the Listener and I would watch from afar, with disbelief, as fish would leave the sea, evolve their fins into feet, and start walking on the beaches. I would always ask them if they were entirely sure about what they were doing. Still, those animals would ignore me as they confidently left behind their aquatic existence to become amphibians, and afterwards, reptiles.

I would gain a sense of relief as we saw mammals abandon their land lives, evolve their legs into fins and slink back to their original ocean home. The evolution of those animals, in response to their ever-changing environments, filled me with a sense of calm and inspiration. Just like Small had to become me, 'Aqua Maddas', to survive, many other animals had to become something different, also to carry on in an unpredictable world.

I came to realise that time in the Listener's boat was different from time everywhere else. Creatures would emerge, thrive, and then become extinct in what would probably feel like a week in human time. I remember asking the Listener about that, but his reply would simply be a confused shrug before playing a different record. That would also be his response whenever I asked him about why he could not speak.

We passed through one era, thankfully quite briefly, when the world was unpleasantly cold. However, our record player blessed us with interesting clapping, drumming and chant music when we passed icy landmasses. I was at first curious about who was making this music, but then my attention was stolen by groups of playful penguins in the Southern Ocean that thrived when the planet was frozen.

I braved the frosty oceans so that I could swim amongst graceful groups of penguins as they glided effortlessly through the water. Sometimes I waddled with them when they were out of the ocean, inhabiting glaciers, and I made friends by gifting them with fresh fish.

I also remember that there was a long period when the planet became so warm that most of the ice melted and the oceans outnumbered the islands. Much of the rocky land had become submerged in a flood that seemed to want to claim the entire planet. To our surprise, during that time, the Listener and I caught sight of another boat! All our energy was then suddenly spent trying to steer our vessel towards theirs.

"Who are they?! Hello!! I want to meet you!" I remember yelling as I pushed the Listener to help us get to them. The poor little guy shrugged his shoulders – no music could guide us. I remember trying to use my make-shift spears as oars to steer the boat and then spending most of my remaining 'high' energy trying to move our boat against the tides.

No matter how much effort we made, the other boat drifted far away from us before disappearing from our view entirely."

"Is that when you experienced your first 'low'?" the Therapist asked, continually jotting down notes.

"I had been 'low' for a long time on my Island, but that time when the other boat had disappeared, that was my first 'low' after escaping. I had used up all my strength and power and had exhausted the Listener's capability of reaching a vanishing target. All I wanted to do was to collapse in a heap on the wooden deck of the boat and sleep for millennia, trusting that the ocean would take me to where I needed to go..."

"So, I am sorry, Susan, that I act unpredictably and dance before the storm," Maddas concluded with their apology. "It can be difficult for me to switch off."

"It just amazes me how you have so much energy in the first place," Susan grinned worriedly before whispering to a nearby Nurse, "a stronger dose next time."

Maddas, the Storyteller

"All you need to do is take these seedlings and plant them in the holes. It's as easy as pie," hurried the stern, matter-of-fact Gardener. They were the boss of the mental health ward's outside spaces and communicated that with everything about them. "The yard isn't going to make itself pretty!" she bellowed.

Patient Seven, who often felt more comfortable outside than trapped inside buildings for long periods, felt calm in the Gardener's company and hoped that she felt the same way. However, it was difficult to read the Gardener's emotions, if any.

"Would you like a conversation?" Maddas asked her awkwardly whilst patting fresh soil over the roots of a strawberry plant seedling.

"Yes, but not with you," the Gardener answered abruptly. "I don't talk to patients."

"I'm not a patient, though. I am more of a creature. I've been held here against my will," Patient Seven replied in a confusingly gleeful tone.

"...And I've definitely been warned about *you*, Maddas" the Gardener put forward again – her social walls as bleak and impenetrable as the grey stone barriers around the facility. "You are well-known here as 'Maddas, the Storyteller'."

"So, does that mean you don't like stories?" Maddas frowned. "Look, I'm not really into Gardening, Beverly," Maddas squinted, reading the Gardener's tiny scrawl on their name card before carrying on. "But I thought I'd make an effort since that's your 'thing'. It is only fair that you try to appreciate my stories. They can be very entertaining."

"I like stories, but not yours. Yours are all nonsense and make-believe," Beverly replied, even more tersely than before. "Just plant the seedlings."

"Aren't all good stories full of nonsense and make-believe though?" Patient Seven carried on with the shameless determination that probably got them locked in the facility in the first place. "Stories, by their very definition, may contain elements of truth or fantasy in various balances. At least give me a chance."

"As long as you can garden while you talk," she sighed, looking a little upset at being defeated.

"As I may have mentioned to you before, I used to travel in a little magical boat with my friend, the Listener, who would steer our cabin cruiser by playing eerily relevant music to wherever we needed to go. However, one of our adventures began with a good stretch of silence. Sometimes the only music we required was the gentle sound of the waves in the calm ocean deserts that we would drift through.

There was one ocean that will captivate the soul, I hope, forever. The waters were as clear as unspoilt glass, offering us a window into a magnificent aquatic paradise below. However, in certain places, a rich red hue on the water's surface provided us with a fascinating filter. Interesting fact, Bev, if I may call you that?"

"No, call me Beverly," the Gardener snapped.

"Sure. Fascinating fact, Beverly, but that red hue is due to a bacterium called *Trichodesmium erythraeum.* Since you're into plants, I figured that you might be interested in biology," Maddas grinned, eyes wide open in the hope of a connection.

"...That is quite interesting," huffed Beverly, as if suffering a minor defeat. "The Red Sea is a wonderful place. You are fortunate to have been able to visit there."

"It is captivating. I agree I was incredibly fortunate," Maddas nodded, smiling, and uplifted by the feeling of relating to someone.

"I was a very lucky monster. I swam with gigantic turtles – they seemed to be at ease with another spiky, scaly creature despite me being a stranger to the scenery. Spiny lionfish, vibrant, blue-spotted rays and friendly hammerhead sharks also enjoyed my company as I drifted around the reefs and reeds. It was such a beautiful place that I had forgotten the desperation I felt at not being able to contact the people on a faraway boat some time ago.

However, something happened at the Red Sea, which shook me to my core. As I explored the ocean floor, I suddenly placed my webbed hands and feet on land! It was not regular land, I must add. It was no beach or island. It was land that had suddenly appeared where it had not been before. A temporary pathway had emerged that had separated the ocean.

At first, I stood in the centre of the path, almost frozen to the spot by my disbelief. I heard some commotion, though, which startled me. Instinctively, I slipped back through one of the ocean 'curtains' and hid behind a large piece of coral. Whilst I disappeared and camouflaged with my surroundings, I gazed in awe as an enormous crowd of human beings hurried through the ocean pathway.

The people walked past, 'through' the ocean and I was there, wishing I could walk beside them. I wanted so much to step out and greet them, and I would have asked them about where they were going. I yearned so much to understand their stories and wished that I were a part of their story, instead of being a weird creature watching them from a hiding place."

Patient Seven paused, noticing that Beverly's face had turned an odd mosaic of white and red. They displayed a wave of anger that could have almost earned her a place in the ward.

"Stop talking to me," she gasped. "You ungodly creature! You devil!"

"Woah, OK," Maddas winced. "Sea Devil has been my name for a short stretch of history, but I don't think I qualify to be the actual Devil. He seems to be very important and has a lot of responsibilities, unlike me."

"Get away from me! Stop talking to me!" Beverly screamed.

"Is everything OK?" interrupted Susan, the Therapist, who hurried suddenly to the scene.

"No!" growled Beverly.

"I don't know…" Maddas shrugged.

"Perhaps it's time for you to go inside, for your medication, Maddas?" Susan suggested gently yet sternly, guiding Patient Seven back into the building.

"OK," Maddas agreed sadly.

Patient Seven slumped on their bed, feeling a complete loss of motivation and energy as they accepted the fact that they had been locked in their dormitory again. They sat up and attempted to get the attention of the stocky male Nurse that sat calmly, guarding the door. The Nurse half acknowledged Maddas's hand-waving before determinedly ignoring them to focus on some commotion in the hallway.

There, Maddas sat in their hospital room, watching for hours as people passed their door's window. They remembered that moment in the Red Sea again and began to re-experience the feeling of being an outsider, watching a tribe of people that they wished and prayed so much to join.

Maddas recalled that the people who walked through the Red Sea looked starving, traumatised and beyond exhausted, but they had something that Maddas yearned for almost every day. The people who walked that ocean pathway had each other. They had company, support, and a sense of belonging. Despite having had the Listener for company at that time, there was something akin to 'family' that

Maddas desired so much that they even considered giving up their ocean home.

"So, it's back to square one," Maddas sighed before crushing a white pill with their clawed hand. They stood up, licked the medication dust from their hand and then placed their palm to the window of their locked door. That moment brought back memories of when the Red Sea water closed off the ocean pathway, much like the rapid closing of a door to the world of humanity.

Maddas stumbled backwards and lay down on their hospital bed. They reminisced about swimming up to the Listener's boat after witnessing the parting of the ocean.

"I remember jumping aboard that boat and being incredibly erratic. The Listener scratched his head as I paced around the deck in utter confusion," Maddas muttered to themselves.

"Did you see that? Did you see those people walk through the ocean? Did that happen?" I questioned energetically, holding the Listener's fluffy, unsettled head up close to mine.

The Listener shrugged, stepped away from me and decided to search through their cardboard box for the next record."

"Does it even matter that it happened?" present-day Maddas sighed to themselves, slipping into a medication-induced but much-needed slumber. "Does something have to be completely real, when all that matters is how it makes you feel?"

"Are you OK?" asked the Nurse, suddenly entering the room.

"I'm OK," Maddas slurred with a dopey smile. "Beverly liked my Red Sea bacteria fact."

A Woman Swam Alone

Maddas did not get on well with the idea of sleep, especially at night. Nightfall was when the best and worst of humanity came into play. Patients paced the corridors, also un-entranced by slumber. Nurses would appear suddenly at Maddas's door to check on them. The Nurses had Patient Seven's best interest at heart, but their presence would startle Maddas awake, and no amount of medication seemed to be able to lull them back to relaxation.

Maddas would often spend the quiet time of the early morning sitting and reading books in the communal area. They would keep the Night Nurses company as they hid under their blankets, trying their best to get any form of rest on the uncomfortable chairs.

When the sunrise began to greet the mental health ward, Maddas would sit on a bench in the outside space and watch the sky, listen to birds sing and feel moderately at peace. However, it did nothing for the loneliness that Patient Seven often felt.

They looked back through the windows that separated the outside space from the communal area. At one of the breakfast tables sat a young girl, all by herself. She was wearing a fuchsia-coloured fluffy jumper, and a silken, magenta headscarf covered her jet-black hair. She caught Maddas's gaze and glanced away shyly before becoming focussed on her sketch pad.

Maddas took some deep breaths and summoned the confidence to step back inside the ward and attempt to make a friend.

"Hello!" Patient Seven boomed, sitting down next to the girl.

"Hi," she squeaked timidly, her gaze still fixated on her drawing. It was a very detailed, beautiful sketch of a bird - possibly a dove.

"Your drawing is amazing," Maddas gasped.

A window suddenly opened next to them, revealing a food counter. Nurses behind the counter began to toast bread and prepare breakfast for the patients.

"Ooh, food!" Maddas cheered as they gazed at Nurses piling packets of jam into a bowl. They looked back towards the girl to find that she had disappeared entirely, along with her art. A hungry Nurse replaced them at the table.

"Early birds, eh?" the Nurse beamed with a warm, broad smile.

"Hi there, Agwe?" Maddas grinned back, reading the Nurse's name card. "A girl was sitting here just a minute ago, am I right?"

"Oh yes, that's our 'Dawn Drawer'. Always here before breakfast, but she never eats anything or talks to anyone. Go and get yourself some toast Maddas, don't take it personally," Agwe suggested.

Maddas sat back down next to Agwe, whilst they crunched on jam and toast.

"I scare people away all the time," Maddas sighed as tears soaked their bread.

"You are a little bit scary, though," Agwe chuckled.

"I can't do much about my spikes and blue-green skin," Maddas muttered. "I don't mean any harm, though. I can try to be more normal again."

"You're 'Maddas the Storyteller' but remember that you're not the only person here who has a story to tell," Agwe replied - his brown eyes gleaming with a gentle, knowing gaze.

"I know, that's why I like to meet people. I love to get lost in their stories and learn about their adventures. When I was on the boat with the Listener, we met a lot of fascinating people, eventually."

"Come on, tell me a story over breakfast, Maddas," Agwe invited.

"After I had glimpsed humanity from a distance at the Red Sea, I was determined to make contact and build some friendships. Our little boat appeared beside various human ships for many centuries. When I boarded boats in the Mediterranean Sea, I faced spears, bows and arrows. Axes and swords met me on beautifully built Viking ships in the North Sea. We travelled to the Pacific, and vessels full of cannons prevented us from going anywhere near humans. The Atlantic introduced me to more fire, rifles, and shotguns. I tried to make friends with every seafaring human that I could. Even on the ones not built for combat, people wanted me off their ships. Despite my gifts of fish, ornate pebbles and gigantic shells, my presence shook people to the core and drove them to attack me.

Centuries of rejection just made my skin thicker and more impervious to weapons. However, after the Listener forced me to hear the many songs about me which mentioned 'Sea Demon', 'Ocean Devil' or 'Marine Monster', I felt it was time to reflect on my approach. Perhaps I could adapt, as I had always done.

I just wanted a normal conversation. I yearned to find out why humans had so many weapons and were always trying to hurt each other. My aim was never to harm or scare anyone. Perhaps it was my appearance or over-eager body-language that signalled a threat to people.

For a little while, I took a break from humanity and left the Listener's boat to explore the Great Barrier Reef. My days in the dazzling, unblurred underwater paradise of the reef involved picturesque rainforests of coral. It was a magnificent labyrinth of life, and the scenery was profound. I gazed at corals of every colour, including 'trees' of red, decorated with yellow, green and purple hues.

I swooped through enormous shoals of fish, impressed at their ability to form whirlpools, and avoid giant, intimidating wrasse. One of my favourite memories was of a friendly family of dugong that let me spend some time with them as they hoovered the ocean floor.

Once I had had my fill of the reef, I rested and meditated on the deck of the Listener's boat. He played a record with energetic chanting that almost masked the sound of splashes near to our craft. When I sat up to examine where the splashing was coming from, there I saw her. A woman swam alone, towards us. There was no sign of any ships nearby. She was just head down and powered by a determination to go somewhere.

"Hello!" I cried. "Do you need a boat?"

She looked up at me and our boat and was so shocked that she almost choked on a mouthful of seawater.

The Listener and I helped her up the little ladder and onto the deck, and we rushed to get her drinking water and fresh fish to eat. For a long while, she sat, exhausted. Her tongue had swollen from swallowing seawater, and it was difficult for her to talk for some time. She sipped at water slowly and cautiously accepted some of our food.

I tried not to stare, and in fact, the Listener frowned at me for glancing at her too much, but she was the first human I had ever truly met. Her hair was long, wavy, and dark brown. She was wearing a sea-soaked dress with unique patterns of red, black, and white. Unlike any other human I had met before, her chin displayed an intricate black tattoo.

"Where are you swimming towards?" I asked.

"Anywhere else," she gasped, holding her head in her hands.

I sat in silence with no idea what to say or do. The Listener patted me on the shoulder as if to tell me to try harder at relating to our guest.

"Ah, so you're swimming *away* from something?"

"Yes," she confirmed.

"My name is Aqua Maddas, Maddas for short. I have some experience in escaping from tough places. What's your name?"

"Nyree," she said softly, slowly raising her head and letting her chestnut eyes meet mine. "Are you...Tangaroa?!" she cried.

"No, I'm Maddas," I corrected. It did not seem to help. To her, I was someone else.

"Where would you like to go? There are a lot of wonderful islands, not too far from here. You can choose which one you want to be your new home?" I suggested.

She paused for a long while, deep in thought. She gazed at the sea, at her hands and her clothes. She chuckled as she recognised the music from the record player.

"I know what I must do," she roared suddenly. "Tangaroa has come to find me to remind me of who I am and where I belong!"

"I'm not...um. My name is Maddas," I tried again.

"All my life, I've been so scared of all the battles fought on my Island. So many people are starving, dying, and being killed. But perhaps the answer is to turn our heads to the ocean and become better at fishing, rather than having to fight in a war," she explained. "I just got so upset with my family and my tribe, I didn't know what to do, so I dived into the ocean and swam away, hoping for answers or a better life."

"I mean, I can completely understand your decision there," I nodded, listening intently, and being watched by the Listener as he assessed my ability to listen.

"I have made my decision. I want to go back to Aotearoa!" she bellowed powerfully. "I will tell my tribe to look to the sea for food before waging war on another tribe. If that does not work, I will die fighting beside the ones that I love!"

"Wow...OK," I shuddered. "You want to go back, Nyree? Even though you might die if you do?"

"Is that not what you are telling me Tangaroa?!" she cried, standing up suddenly and exhibiting an intimidatingly muscular physique.

I remember glancing at the Listener, trying to work out if he was for or against the idea. He shrugged and played another record of chant music whilst I wrestled with a barrage of various, complicated emotions. I was scared that if we delivered her back to her original island, Aotearoa, that she would end up back in a dangerous situation of potential warfare. However, in all honesty, the emotion that I had the most difficulty facing was envy.

I had run away from my Island of the Fallen, never to look back. I had escaped into the beauty of the ocean and lost myself in trying to connect with the complicated creature that was humanity. There had been no warning that through such a connection, I would have to face some harsh truths about myself. Was her bravery highlighting my cowardice? Was her strength reminding me of how weak I was underneath all my scary spikes?

"Will you take me there? I will swim back if you don't," she cut in, forcing me to stop my selfish introspection.

"If you are sure you want to go back, we will do our best to take you back to Aotearoa," I sighed, gulping down my emotions. "Even if it brings me pain thinking that you might get killed, I support what you want to do, Nyree."

"This music that you're playing - it's the music of my tribe," she swooned, dancing to the rhythm and singing along to the words. It was incredible to see such a transformation from a person in peril to an animated woman, confident in every move and word of her dance. She even attempted to teach me how to perform a 'haka', although my big, webbed feet and lack of coordination resulted in an embarrassing display. It was worth it just to make Nyree and the Listener chuckle.

We arrived at the North side of Aotearoa, now known as New Zealand, and delivered her to the beach near her tribal home. We were very cautious not to let our boat get stuck on land, but she was able to paddle back to her family with ease. Before we left, she looked back at us and cried out.

"Thank you, Tangaroa! I will make sure our tribe sings songs about you for many generations!"

"My name is Maddas!" I cried back, but she had already disappeared from our sight.

The Listener played the album labelled 'Aqua Maddas' again. There had been no change to the number of songs about me being a 'Sea Devil' or a 'Sea Demon'. The album 'Tangaroa', however, featured songs about a great, heroic, and generous Sea God.

"Sometimes being a good friend means supporting someone, even if they remind you of your insecurities," I sighed to the Listener. "And sometimes it involves not taking any credit for your kindness."

"Did you find out what happened to Nyree in the end?" Agwe asked Patient Seven intently.

"At that time in my adventures, I had an intense phobia of land, especially one with a proud history of warrior culture," Maddas explained. "But I like to think that whatever happened, she was in command of her destiny. She could have swum away and lived on one of the many paradise islands we had encountered in the Pacific. Those Chatham Islands seemed nice; she could have gone there. However, she bravely chose to go back to her family. Perhaps she chose diplomacy or living off the ocean. Perhaps she fought. Whatever she chose, I was happy that I was able to enjoy her company and be a part of her story, even for a short while."

The alarm suddenly screeched through the complex. Agwe thanked Patient Seven and left his unfinished breakfast to deal with an emergency. Maddas hoped that they would be able to tell a little bit of Agwe's busy and chaotic story one day.

A Tailor

The next day, Maddas sat beside the Dawn Drawer girl again, still determined to make a friend. After at least two minutes of painfully awkward silence, the girl surprised Maddas by gifting them with a sketch. She even cautiously shared her colouring pencils with Patient Seven.

"Ooh, a pirate ship?!" Maddas exclaimed, admiring the skilful artwork before them. "It's wonderfully drawn! Um, what's your name?"

The girl remained silent whilst focussed on her own pirate ship drawing.

"You know, I've met a few pirates. They're not all skulls and crossbones," Maddas mentioned.

"Hmm," she replied with an air of disbelief.

"I'm telling the truth," Maddas pressed.

"So, what are pirates like then?" she asked, resisting the urge to make eye-contact with Patient Seven.

"The first pirate I met was very well-dressed. You'd have got on well with him."

The girl blushed and fiddled with the magenta headscarf that covered her black, silky hair.

"It was my friend, the Listener, who found him. This time it was not through playing any records on our boat. We had drifted into a thick fog and were barely able to see anything. However, the Listener had caught a sound from somewhere. I thought we were just chasing silence, but then I heard a melodic, beautiful singing voice pierce through the calm.

Amidst the mists, we found a tiny desert island of mostly sand and rock, with a man sitting on it, singing to himself as he tried to repair a small wooden boat that was no longer fit for sea-faring. I had a sense that he had been waiting patiently for us. Indeed, he was not surprised to see the Listener. His attire was slightly weather-beaten, but he wore a long, fine, cyan-blue robe over an inner, cream-coloured garment. His curly, dark-brown hair was wrapped in an elegant, turquoise head-dress.

The Listener leapt off the boat and embraced the gentlemen. They greeted each other with friendly cheek-to-cheek kisses.

"I didn't realise you had friends?" I frowned. "All this time, I've been yearning to connect with humans, and you had friends I could meet all along?"

The Listener looked at me sternly, commanding that I show more grace.

"Amigo, who is this fascinating beast?" the man asked the Listener.

"My name is Aqua Maddas - call me Maddas for short," I introduced, holding out a webbed claw to shake his hand.

"Antonio Cortissos - please call me Cortissos," he smiled charmingly. His intense brown eyes were inspecting every inch of my being before turning back to the Listener.

"Thank you for hearing my songs, Amigo," he exclaimed. "I need some help from you. Can you tell me, am I still surrounded by attacking ships? My telescope is powerful, but not enough to see through the fog."

The Listener inspected the slightly cracked telescope that Cortissos revealed from an inner pocket in his voluminous robe. Remembering that he had no experience in mending telescopes, the Listener gave it back to Cortissos with a clueless shrug.

"Will you help me get my ships back? I was attacked and forced to flee and hide on my Island of Fog."

"We can certainly try," I agreed, staring at the Listener to understand his response.

The Listener thought for a minute and nodded. We welcomed Cortissos onto our little boat and travelled away from the island, through the fog. I had a feeling that Cortissos had some more secrets hidden up his well-tailored sleeves.

As the mists dispersed, they revealed the carcasses of three wooden ships that had been ravaged by fire. The flames of one were slowly extinguished by it sinking into the ocean - its hull punctured beyond repair.

"It's all gone!" Cortissos wailed. "These were the last three vessels of my wealth - all of it plundered. My crew are dead! They destroyed all my ships! It's all gone!"

"Cortissos, I'm sorry that your ships got destroyed," I mused. "But it's not all gone; you are still alive. I sense that within you, you are a lot more powerful than you seem. I feel like you are somehow connected to the sea as I am."

"That is true. To the sea, I am connected," Coritssos grinned, his expression switching from one of despair to one of pride. "I come from a long line of Sephardic merchants. My ancestors and I charted the globe, selling fine goods from Portugal and Spain. Seafaring is in my blood. Or, it was, until I lost all of my ships."

"You are still here though," I cut in, trying to keep Cortissos from falling back into depression. "You're wearing such amazing clothes. Your gown is a wonderful colour."

"Indeed, seafaring is just one part of my trade. You see, I wanted to give up my life on the ocean so that I could pursue my dream of being a tailor. I have made robes like this for many people and almost came close to living my dream. But alas, I have been pushed out to sea again. My people, the Sephardim, were exiled from our homes. So many of my family and friends perished. I took to the sea again, ferrying my family and riches to new countries. This journey was going to be my last voyage."

"You surviving means that you may indeed get to live your dream, in a new place. I'm sure you will get another ship, probably more," I tried, feeling moved by Cortissos's story.

"You're right. You are absolutely right. I do not feel quite alive right now, though," Cortissos nodded with a sigh, before turning to the Listener and asking for a request. "Please my Amigo, play some Ladino songs for me. Play them loud. I need to cling to something that may be lost forever."

The Listener paused for a moment before playing the melodic 'A La Una Yo Nasi' at the highest volume. Cortissos exhaled slowly before appearing to meditate. He looked out to the sea and seemed to be waiting for something. A wide grin radiated underneath the waterfall of tears from his energetic eyes. Another ship appeared on the horizon.

"The *Santo Cristo*," he growled. "One of the ships that hunted me."

"Do you think perhaps, this music has made us a bit of a target?" I frowned worriedly at the Listener who shrugged as the energising song 'Fel Shara' started playing.

"Exactly, keep playing," Cortissos ordered. "Louder!"

The record player was at its highest setting but appeared to respond to Cortissos' shout by becoming even louder.

"I didn't realise your record player responded to voice commands?" I uttered to the Listener before looking back towards Cortissos, who had entirely vanished from our boat. There was no sign that he had dived into the sea or swam towards the oncoming ship.

He had left behind his telescope, however. Through it, I was able to catch a glimpse of Cortissos climbing up the side of the Santo Cristo ship - his robe fluttering in the wind like a brilliant blue flag. The vessel itself was full of large crates of cargo, and it was a miracle that it had not sunk. Some of the containers had the word 'Cortissos', noticeably scrawled on the side.

"Maybe I should help our friend?" I suggested. "He's going to get himself killed."

I dive-bombed into the sea and torpedoed myself towards the ship.

"I need you to talk to the Captain, Maddas!" Cortissos bellowed at me.

"What should I say?" I asked, using my sharp claws to climb swiftly up the sea-soaked wood to meet with Cortissos.

"Anything you want, Amigo," Cortissos laughed mysteriously.

I leapt onto the deck, bracing myself for an inevitable attack.

"Um, hello," I smiled awkwardly, as most of the crew froze in surprise at seeing me. "Can you give my friend his stuff back please?"

"Um Monstro!" they shouted at me, grabbing hooked-guns and muskets, ready to shoot me down. I ran to the helm of the ship, hoping to speak with the captain, but he too was yelling 'Monstro!' at me. Amongst the chaos, I had completely lost sight of Cortissos.

That was until he appeared suddenly in the middle of the ship's deck.

"You made a grave error by taking this cargo from me," Cortissos grinned with a wry laugh as he raised his arms.

As if by telekinesis, the cargo boxes opened suddenly at his command. Out of them flew dozens of robes of various colours that moved by themselves. They seemed to dance around Cortissos in a circle, the sleeves waving to match Cortissos's gestures.

"All the men, women and children I made clothes for, that were killed in the expulsion - parts of their souls still cling to the cloth fibres of these magical robes," Cortissos cheered. "May they dance with joy; may they have their revenge before they find their peace."

"What?!" I cried as I witnessed an entire ship's crew become completely overrun and outfought by a well-dressed army of invisible souls. They seemed to be undefeatable, and even if torn by knives and swords, the robes were able to wind their sleeves around the arms and necks of their foes. Anyone who tried to attack Cortissos or his garments were pushed and tripped by swift sweeps of material, sending them overboard to the cold waters below.

"Captain of the Santo Cristo, you will leave this ship with your crew in the small lifeboats, or face the wrath of the most elegant ghost army this world will ever see," Cortissos put forward, facing the Captain with a stare that could freeze the hearts of most mortal men.

"Please, don't take my ship. We were just taking care of your cargo. We never meant you any harm," pleaded the Captain, bowing to Cortissos on his hands and knees.

"You never meant any harm by burning my ships and killing my crew? You never meant any harm by stealing from my family? Or standing by as so many of us were killed and forced out from our homes?" Cortissos snarled, reaching for a hidden dagger from within his robe.

"Cortissos, is this the kind of revenge you want?" I interrupted, trying to get between Cortissos's blade and a Captain that was about to see his last.

"You don't understand Maddas!" Cortissos shouted, still clinging to the Captain by his shirt.

"Don't think I don't know about you, Maddas, o Monstro da Água!"

"Cool, is that my name in Portuguese?" I asked.

"Don't interrupt me!" Cortissos bellowed. "I know that you left your Cursed Island out of your own will. My family were banished. We are rejected, persecuted, and expelled! We are doomed to Exodus for eternity, but the Sea does not part for my family or me. It is myself that must master the sea, in any way that I can."

"I think I know what you mean. I think I saw the sea part for some people a while back," I mused, getting slightly distracted.

"No, you didn't, idiota," Cortissos snapped. "Leave me to either take this man's life, or take his ship, or perhaps both."

"Are you sure you want to take this path?"

"It is not me who chose this path. I am just trying to carry my earnings and my robes to my family in Amsterdam. That is if they even reached Amsterdam at all. Whoever steals my robes brought their fate onto themselves," Cortissos argued. "I didn't choose piracy!"

"Does their fate have to be death? You're a creative man, surely you can think of revenge more fitting than death?"

"Listen to the strange, talking fish person, Cortissos," the Captain pleaded. "You have taken my crew, you can have my ship, just don't take my life!"

"You're right. I am not someone who takes pleasure in killing," Cortissos sighed. "I will be generous. Not only will I let you and your surviving crew leave in one of your tiny boats, but I will also give you one of my robes. You may want to throw it away, but it will be the best thing you will ever own, so you will not. If you ever try to take from my people again, you will be suffocated by the cloth in an instant."

"You are most generous, Cortissos. I will not forget you. We will sing your name for many centuries," the Captain cried, tears falling from his eyes.

"Ah, it's only one of my many names. I will probably change it when I get to the new country," muttered Cortissos as he wrapped the Captain in one of his well-woven silk robes and sent him off the ship in a small lifeboat.

"You were right, Maddas, I would get another ship," Cortissos grinned, taking control of the wheel at the helm.

"Thank you Maddas, and thank you, my Amigo, for all of your help, and providing me with the perfect music for this moment!" he called out to the Listener, who was still playing Ladino songs whilst waiting for me to return to our boat.

"Travel safely to your new life in Amsterdam, Cortissos," I beamed, embracing the enigmatic gentleman before preparing to dive back into the ocean. "You will find a better life, one in which you can be a tailor and bring your incredible, magical fashion to wherever you live next. Won't that be the best revenge of all?"

"It will, Maddas. I will never forget you. The blue and green stripes on your skin and the spikes on your back will inspire the next robe I make. It will be a piece I will call 'o Monstro da Água'."

"Not Aqua Maddas?"

"No. O Monstro da Água," he confirmed.

"OK, bye-bye," I chirped, before jumping off the side of the boat and diving into the ocean. I was elated to feel the cool of the water again after such an overwhelming time on the ship.

"A Despedida!" Cortissos called to us as he sailed away. The Listener and I watched him disappear out of our line of sight, playing 'El Rey Nimrod' at the highest volume out of respect."

"Maybe you should have let him have his revenge," the Dawn Drawer girl commented as she tidied away her colouring pencils and art materials. "It's a good story, though, thank you."

"Anytime," Maddas smiled. "Thank you for listening to me."

"I understand Cortissos's pain right now, as should you," she said sternly. "By being locked in here, we are both society's rejects. My name is Alice, by the way."

Patient Seven watched Alice as she hurried away and back to her room before breakfast was about to be served. Maddas reflected on what Alice had said, before crushing the piece of paper with the pirate drawing on it and throwing it at the wall. They too went back to their room, feeling too emotional to eat toast.

Pirate Queen

Sometimes the mental health ward Nurses would confine Patient Seven to their room for various reasons, including displaying sudden bursts of emotion. The Nurse, Agwe would sit on a small bench outside Maddas's room, guarding them and checking on them every ten minutes or so. Maddas would lie on their unmade bed and gaze at the white ceiling, as well as the cream-coloured, art-less walls. They often felt as though the room was becoming smaller with every minute that they spent in it.

"I feel like I'm in a cage," Maddas gasped, opening the door. "This reminds me of the time when someone put me in an actual cage."

"Come sit and have a little bit of air, but you must go back in afterwards Maddas," Agwe stated softly but with a firm tone to his deep, mellow voice.

"OK," Patient Seven sighed before sitting carefully beside Agwe, making sure that the Nurse was at a safe distance from their spiky shoulders.

"So, when were you put in a cage?" Agwe asked.

"It was a cage from my point of view, but it was actually gift-wrapping. I was captured by a fierce pirate who wanted to give me as a gift to a Queen who controlled the seas," Maddas began.

"OK Maddas, tell me what happened, make my morning," Agwe chuckled, sipping on a cup of tea that he had hidden beside him.

"After the very intense encounter with Cortissos, I needed to recharge my spirits and explore the underwater of the Alboran Sea, in the West of the Mediterranean. I glided through the calm, colourful waters, greeting beautifully striped painted comber fish, brilliant red starfish, and fascinating large jellyfish before making friends with a pod of playful bottlenose dolphins.

I had the best time socialising with cetaceans, and dolphins would usually provide the best company. Their language of clicks and whistles is impenetrable, but they will laugh at your jokes should you try to speak with them. At least, I felt as though they were laughing *with* me. They just appreciate the simple things in life. For instance, they will play catch with a piece of sponge for ages or have competitions to see who can blow gigantic bubbles underwater.

My joyful time with the dolphins ended when I noticed that a much larger ship had approached our boat. I shot up through the water and re-joined the Listener as he stood, paralysed in fear before an intimidating man with a turban, reddish coloured-beard, and a cutlass sword. What was even more striking was that his left arm was made entirely of metal. He had boarded our boat from a hooked rope, latched onto the side of our cabin cruiser.

"Oh wow, what is this?" the man exclaimed as he set his eyes on me. "And I thought that the music machine was the best thing I would set eyes upon today."

"Hi, I am Aqua Maddas, it's nice to meet you," I greeted, attempting to make friends, despite the fear.

"Sea Monster, it is nice to meet you! You will call me Baba. Now, you are coming with me!" he ordered, trying to grab me. I pushed him away, defending myself from his sword with the spikes on my elbows. As he staggered back, I bared my sharp teeth and made sure to stand between Baba and the Listener. Before I could even try to unhook our boat from the enemy ship, Baba drew his sword and pointed the blade towards the gills in my neck.

"You will come with me, or one of my many ships will blow this tiny boat with a cannonball," Baba threatened, gesturing to the arrival of at least five more ships.

"I'll go along with it. Get yourself to safety. I can handle this, I think," I muttered to the Listener who was still shaking.

With swords pointed towards me from Baba and his crew, as well as cannons still aimed at our boat, I climbed nervously up a small wooden ladder on the side of Baba's ship. Stares and jeers greeted me whilst Baba pushed me into a rusty cage. Trying to think positively, I was thankful that I was in a cell by myself. In the other prisons on the ship, there were many angry, terrified people crammed together in groups.

Concentrating hard, I tried my best to use any strength that I still had to summon a storm. I had a feeling though that those pirates would not be easily beaten by violent weather, however.

"You may be a Sea Monster, but in these waters, I am the only person you should be afraid of," Baba laughed at me through the cage bars.

"That's not completely true, Captain," one of his crew interjected. "You are feared but, it is She who controls the seas here."

"Yes, thank you," grumbled Baba. "This creature will be a valuable gift for my Queen."

There was nothing much I could do apart from stay calm and build my energy reserves so that I could devise an escape plan. So, I simply fell asleep in the cage. The journey from the sea to the Queen's palace was a complete blur. I just curled up in a corner and dozed as the crew carried me from the ship, through a city of white houses and mountains in the background. That was all I managed to glimpse in between snoring my way through captivity.

The situation brought back memories of feeling imprisoned on my Island, except this time, it was cold metal bars and savage humans rather than grasping vines and sinking sand.

"A gift for you, al-Hurra," Baba boomed as he dropped my cage suddenly on the stone floor of an impressive palace building. I woke up suddenly and inspected my surroundings. The floor boasted a striking, black, and white square pattern, much like a gigantic chess set. Columns decorated by intricate gold artwork supported an imposing and extraordinarily white ceiling. Everything seemed to be embellished by lavish gold detail that glistened behind bright fire-lit lanterns.

"What an incredible cave," I muttered to myself.

"This creature as well as all those valuable captives?" an authoritative female voice replied. "You out-do yourself Oruç."

It seemed as though Baba responded to many different names.

"Um, thanks for not killing me I guess," I mumbled to Baba as he and his crew excused themselves from the palace. I was left in the cage, pretty much alone with a Queen and her surrounding courtiers.

"Hmm, it speaks," the Queen smiled as she inspected the cage. She wore a luxurious red dress with gold-coloured, low-hanging sleeves. A golden, silk veil covered her ebony hair, and jet-black eyeliner enhanced her striking chestnut eyes. She carried with her an aura of power and presence. Honestly, even though I was in a cage, I felt it was an excellent opportunity to meet a very impressive human.

"Um, you seem like a great person. I mean you no harm at all and I don't need to be in a cage," I tried.

"I will decide whether or not you mean me harm," she replied coolly. "What are you?"

"I'm not completely sure of that, but my name is Aqua Maddas. Maddas for short," I greeted.

"Where do you come from?"

"A cursed Island originally, but my home is the sea," I answered flatly, leaving the Listener out of the conversation on purpose. I was worried about whether he was safe at the time.

"Hmm," she murmured, her mind quickly processing the entirety of the situation. She was exceptionally level-headed for someone meeting a sea creature such as myself.

"Well, I have a lot of business to attend to now. We will talk again later," she decided before striding purposefully away.

"Don't just leave me here in this cage! I need water on my skin at some point!" I cried. I could tell that she had heard me and listened, but I soon realised that I was low on her priority list.

So, there I was, trapped in a tiny cage for most of the day with courtiers staring at me. Storm Clouds rumbled above the palace, summoned by the inner rage I felt at being held captive. However, the weather was utterly useless at helping me escape due to me being inside a well-built palace.

Some droplets of rain caught my skin through tiny cracks in the otherwise imposing ceiling. It gave me a minuscule amount of comfort as the parts of my skin that were not scaly or spikey were drying so much that I felt a desperate pain and a yearning for the seawater.

"You can replenish yourself in one of my many fountains," the Queen stated, suddenly appearing in front of me. Although she had a magnificent presence, her footsteps and movement were so quiet, like a panther on a hunt.

"Yes, I need that," I rasped, feeling exhausted by dehydration.

She cautiously opened my cage, still miraculously maintaining her dignity and poise when jostling with the rusty key and padlock. I stayed back for a few seconds, waiting for her to lead the way so as not to startle her. I could see that she was carrying a sword for protection, loosely hidden beneath her long, lavish sleeves. Two armed guards stood by, anticipating my every move.

She led me to a beautifully sculpted fountain in an outside court of the palace. There I slowly immersed myself in the water, feeling the soothing rush of dopamine as I soaked my hair underneath the waterfall. My cracked skin started to heal, and all the pain of dehydration left my body.

"That's so much better," I sighed happily. The storm overhead started to lift.

"So, are you a mermaid, or a merman?" she questioned.

"Mer... person," I answered slowly.

It was such a great feeling to have a human want to know me. I was quizzed for hours and was happy to tell her as much as I could. It was also the first time I had met a human who was not in trouble in some way. However, I could not quite shake off an itchy, uncomfortable feeling from being held captive.

"Can you breathe underwater?" she asked.

"Yes, but I'm not all that interesting," I babbled. "How about you? You're much more interesting than I am."

"That is true. Well, as you will probably know, I rule this city of Tétouan. I've helped this place become the richest, most harmonious it has ever been," she stated with a proud, matter-of-fact manner.

"I didn't know that. Honestly, I don't know anything, but that sounds very impressive," I smiled, finding the Queen's positive attitude infectious and exciting. "The city does look pretty great. Well, from what I could see in between periods of unconsciousness."

"I do not just govern Tétouan. I also control the Mediterranean Sea by my strategic associations with privateers like Baba, whom you had the pleasure of meeting earlier."

"Yes, pleasure," I sneered.

"You, a person of the sea, should have heard my name? I am known as the 'Pirate Queen', and as the woman most feared in these waters. Many people hate me and want me hanged. It's all a part of being successful," she chuckled with not even a glimpse of worry to her tone.

"I've not met many humans. A lot of them seem to want to harm me too, and I don't see myself as being very successful. I get laughed at all the time by the dolphins," I chattered, attempting to lighten the mood.

She laughed, and it was music to my ears. I felt so alive at that moment that I made a human being feel happiness, even if it were only for a fleeting second, and not long before I would have to go back into my cage.

"I'm sorry, Maddas, I must interrupt our conversation. I need to rule my people. When I feel that I can trust you, I will no longer cage you. Until then," she sighed before her guards led me back to my metal box.

"Well, it was nice to talk," I mumbled as she strode away.

I slumped onto the floor of the cage and felt joy from connecting with such an incredible person. However, I also experienced despair from being stuck on land. I missed the ocean and the Listener so much that my emotions brought another heavy thunderstorm to the city.

The next evening, the Queen led me to the same water fountain for a small splash of freedom and more delightful conversation. I sighed contentedly as my skin met water again, and as always, tried to keep an upbeat mood.

"How many languages can you speak?" she asked me.

"I seem to be able to talk to humans in all their languages. Well, apart from Finnish. That's a tough one," I joked.

"And I thought I was adept at languages. I speak an abundance of tongues. It's one of my many strengths," the Queen declared.

"You're an awe-inspiring person, but honestly you don't have to be your best self around me. I get excited about things like pebbles and bubbles. Being a Queen must be a lot of work already. You can let your hair down in my company," I suggested.

"I cover my hair out of respect to my Muslim beliefs, thank you," she replied strictly. "I am a Queen. I must convey strength, poise and command at all times."

"I'm your captive, and you can be anything you want to be in front of me," I reasoned. "Be whatever makes you happy."

"Happiness is a fleeting emotion. I was happy for a little bit with my first husband. I was perhaps a little happier with my second husband. I mean, he travelled to *me* for the wedding. That is not something that just happens, ever. But Maddas, my heart is tied to this city, and anyone who loves me must respect that. However, I remember when I was a child - I did feel happy when I lived in Granada. That was before my family, and I were banished."

"I'm so sorry," I sympathised.

"Not as sorry as those who try to attack my people or me again," she replied, her tone sliced through the sentimental atmosphere like a sharp dagger.

"Hey, you're not the only person I've met who has felt the pain of banishment. I met a man named Cortissos, who had also been exiled from his country," I mentioned.

"Oh, I know of him - brilliant merchant and tailor," she remarked. "I think I have one of his robes. I hope he and his family are safe."

"What's true is that you are a survivor and an inspiration. After all the trauma, you have become an impressive Queen who fights back."

She softened, and said, "sometimes I wish I could just relax on the beach, with sand between my toes and listen to the calm of the sea."

"Well, maybe you can have that. It's OK to enjoy life and relax, especially when you work so hard for the people of Tétouan."

"No, it's a ridiculous idea. On another topic, I notice that since you have been here, there have been many storms directly above my palace. Are you able to control the weather?"

"Sometimes. It's complicated," I worried, feeling a vital need to regain my freedom which resulted in an energetic thunderclap directly above us.

"Hmm," she thought, seeming unaffected by the noise. "Our fields could use a little rain. Also, a few ships could certainly love a good storm."

At that moment, I was glad that our conversation was cut short by the sound of horns blowing and more guards joining us in the courtyard.

"Al-Hurra, a small army has descended on Tétouan," one of the guards informed.

"Who is leading them?" the Queen asked, remaining calm.

"You're not going to believe this. It's Moulay," they carefully reported.

"Oh, it's just my pesky son-in-law. This battle will not take too long. Let us talk more about your weather powers later, Maddas," she decided, regaining her regal composure before being quickly escorted back into the palace. She had completely forgotten to put me back in the cage, so I decided to make a quick getaway.

I followed the smell of the sea air whilst avoiding all the commotion from soldiers and civilians running about the palace. The inhabitants of Tétouan were so distracted by the prospect of war that no one noticed as I scuttled through the city. Dazzled by the beauty of the busy streets and pristine, white houses, I became utterly lost. With some luck, I managed to find the Martil River, which led out to sea.

Overcome with joy at the river water on my skin and the faint sound of music emanating from a small boat at the mouth of the river, I had escaped captivity and found my way back to the Listener and the welcoming call of the sea. With the sounds of fighting in the background, we swiftly waved goodbye to Tétouan and greeted a pod of dolphins as they chaperoned our exit from the Mediterranean Sea."

"Wow, it sounds as though that Queen was a mighty woman," Agwe exclaimed. "Do you think she survived that attack?"

"According to the music of the time and a few rumours, we found out that her son-in-law took Tétouan from the Queen," Maddas informed. "But a couple of years after, the Listener and I drifted around the South East of the Alboran sea. We kept alert for pirates and stayed away from land for the most part, but we did pass by a beach. On the sand sat a woman who looked very much like the Queen, sitting peacefully and relaxed, enjoying the sand and the sea."

A Better Future

Patient Seven sat in an armchair in the communal area and attempted to read a book whilst enjoying the morning sunlight as it shimmered through the windows. Most of the other patients were at the breakfast area apart from one or two people who sat a few seats away from Maddas. Some were reading, and a few patients were watching others who were trying to read. The Nurse, Agwe quietly shuffled around the area, distributing magazines and books around the tables and shelves.

The unstable tranquillity vanished after a sudden outburst from one of the patients.

"Get out of here!" the patient shouted. He was a man in his fifties and wore a face maroon with rage.

"What?" Maddas mumbled, thinking the man was talking to them.

"Get out of here and go back to Africa!" the patient yelled again. Maddas realised that the man was directing his anger towards Agwe.

"What are you on about?" Maddas argued. "Agwe is Jamaican. Even if he were African, it should not matter! He's a Nurse, and he's helping you!"

"Go back to Jamaica then!" the man carried on, this time adding at least five bizarre racist words that would poison a book if written down.

"Ah, it must be time for your medication, Fergus," Agwe decided, gesturing to one of the other Nurses.

Maddas was astounded at how calm and composed Agwe remained, despite the patient becoming increasingly more incensed. Another Nurse ordered Fergus to take his medication before escorting him to his dormitory room. Agwe sighed to himself, finally left in peace to keep working on making sure the communal space was tidy and ordered.

"Agwe, I am so sorry that happened," Maddas sighed sadly, feeling distressed about what they had witnessed.

"It's nothing," Agwe grinned as if he was using his radiant smile to beam the negativity away. "If I let things like that get me down, I will be locked up in a much worse place than here. With a face like mine, that cannot happen, can it?" he chuckled.

"Wow, yeah," Maddas nodded, inspired by Agwe's self-control. Patient Seven was acutely aware that they seemed to be more upset about the incident than Agwe himself.

"Plus, today is Friday, and it's pay-day! Nothing can bring me down! I'm going to spend that money on my daughter's birthday, and my family will have a weekend of sunshine," Agwe cheered. "Now, which magazine would you like? Here's one about peculiar boats, you'll like that!"

Agwe skipped away from the area and spread his light to everyone else in the facility. Meanwhile, Maddas waited in the communal space in the seat next to where Fergus would usually sit. Like a crocodile lying patiently in wait of its prey, Maddas remained calm and still, but inside their mind, they stirred with a plan of attack.

In the late afternoon, Fergus returned to the communal area and sat in his usual seat. He seemed unphased by the presence of a quietly furious Maddas in the chair next to him, with no idea about what Patient Seven was going to do or say next.

"Fergus, why do you have so much hatred towards Agwe?" Maddas began.

"Agwe? Who?" Fergus replied in a confused manner.

"Him," Maddas gestured towards Agwe who was happily eating an apple and laughing with his colleagues in the breakfast area.

"Well, they don't belong here do they," Fergus sneered. "All these coloured people and immigrants are filling up the country, making the place all dangerous. I'm the only one brave enough to speak out about it. The radio and the newspapers tell me to fight for my country. So, I will do that. Where were you born? You look a bit foreign too."

"You do know that Jamaican people fought with us in World War Two?" Maddas informed, trying to control their anger. "And I am sure you also know that Jamaicans, like most African-Americans, were forced into slavery by the British and other European powers?"

"Hmm," the man thought. It was unclear as to whether he was listening to Maddas or not.

"So when you say, go back to where you came from to Agwe, it means that you completely forget that the slave-traders *took* his ancestors from where they were originally from," Maddas began. "In fact, I recall a time when the Listener and I were very busy in the Atlantic sea..."

"Underwater, the Atlantic Ocean was one of my favourite places to mingle with magnificent whales. Sometimes I would just float below the sea surface and gaze in awe as whales of many different species gathered. Humpback, blue and sperm whales would sometimes congregate to sing and click to each other as well as offer protection and affection to their group.

Their superior senses meant that they would rapidly disperse from the area if they heard the noise of a ship. That was often my cue to get out of the water and back to our boat to spot particular vessels and the cargo they were carrying.

Throughout my life at sea and often watching humans from afar, I had witnessed slavery through the centuries without being able to do much about it. The Listener, with his knowing gaze, repeatedly warned me not to try to meddle in the complex affairs of humans. There was no storm I could summon that would stop certain kinds of cruelty without also injuring both the captors and the people I was trying to save.

That time in the Atlantic was different. There was a monstrous, industrial feel to the inhumanity that I witnessed. The Listener and I watched, astounded, as we saw ships crammed with hundreds of chained souls. We would follow the vessels at a safe distance, keeping an eye out for anyone jumping into the sea to escape. Most of the time, when we tried to rescue these escapees, they were so malnourished, exhausted, and diseased that they perished before we could even haul them onto our boat.

We would escort the few individuals that did survive back to their homeland, making sure that soothing African music emanated from the Listener's record player to lift their spirits. Only a couple of people survived the journey back. Often when our boat met the African shorelines, our feeling of accomplishment from rescuing one or two people would be sunk after seeing the loading of hundreds more chained people onto ships by slave traders.

After years of witnessing this inhumanity, the Listener and I tracked where the ships were going to. We had no real plan, except to work out if there was something we could do. I remember that the Listener would stare at me with a worried expression as I made a couple of spears from dried driftwood, string and with the sharp spikes that grew from my back. Storm clouds would follow our boat, brought from the surging anguish that I felt every time I saw ships full of African prisoners crossing the Atlantic.

Our boat drifted to the Caribbean, wherefrom afar we witnessed thousands of chained Africans working in fields on all the small islands dotted around the beauteous but blighted ocean. We saw people being traded and sold all around the coastlines.

"I am just one small creature. How can I possibly defeat slavery; a monster so much uglier and more complicated than myself?" I pondered.

The sound of hushed African chants, amplified from our record player, brought us near to the South East of Jamaica. So transfixed with thinking about what to do, we did not pay attention when the Earth itself seemed to convulse. We thought it was just the ocean being the tough savage that it could sometimes be, but when we saw parts of the Jamaican coast fall into the sea, we realised that we had steered our way into an earthquake.

A gigantic tsunami seized our tiny boat and sent us on a terrifying surf towards the mainland as it smothered the town. We had seen these giant waves before, but we had never seen one claim a human settlement in the way that it did for Port Royal, Jamaica.

The Listener and I clung to our boat, which was surprisingly resilient when so many other ships became capsized. Once the Earth settled, and the tsunami began to retreat, we quickly looked for any survivors. Amongst the ruined buildings and destroyed ships, we soon became surrounded by a horrific sea of bodies with no sign of life for miles. However, a miracle took our boat to a small wooden raft with a group of survivors clinging on for dear life.

"Help! None of us can swim! Help us before the sharks get us!" we heard a woman scream.

We helped a group of five Africans onto our boat and used rocks and my back spikes to remove the shackles and ropes that had tied their hands and feet together. Noticing open flesh wounds on their backs that were stinging in pain from dried sea salt, we applied seaweed-soaked rags to their backs in the hope it would help to soothe and heal them.

At one point, the Listener gestured very urgently towards the ocean. Small bubbles were rising from the sea. I poked my head under the water and saw that one of the people we had tried to save had accidentally slipped back into the water. Still manacled, he was sure to drown. I quickly dived down and embraced him, shooting him back up to the surface. As I took him in my arms, I noticed more people in shackles sinking to a terrible watery grave.

After pushing the water from the almost drowned man's lungs as he lay on the deck of our boat, I sighed with relief as he coughed up water and regained consciousness.

"This is a nightmare. I can't save everyone," I sobbed, trying to think if there was a way to rescue all the poor people who were not even able to attempt to swim.

The Listener placed his hand on my arm and persuaded me with a knowing expression, to turn my attention from the ocean. He urged me to concentrate on the six people that we had saved.

Still shaking with adrenaline, I shared fresh fish with our guests from a net that I always kept stocked for such emergencies. The Listener steered the boat away from the coast whilst I pondered about what to do next.

"So, do you want to go to Africa?" I asked them.

The Listener put on a record and made a point about making me see the album cover. The picture showed a map of Jamaica and the words 'Music of the Maroons'.

"We need to find a way to get to the Blue Mountains," one of our guests stated. "North East of here."

"Mountains?" I winced. "In all honesty, our speciality is the sea. I've climbed a small hill before, and it was terrible. Even though I have sharp claws, my big, webbed feet are not great for climbing rocks. I would not be able to help protect you and would definitely slow you down."

"If we can get to the river, we can follow it up to the Mountains if we travel at night," another guest suggested.

"We need to get to the Rio Grande river. Can you take us there?" another requested.

"OK. Will that be safe? What's happening in the mountains?" I asked, realising it was a foolish question within seconds. The entire boat fell silent for a few minutes whilst the Listener slapped his face with the palm of his hand in exasperation.

"Who are you?" one man asked me.

"It's Olokun, come to save us!" a woman cried.

"Olokun, the Yoruba sea god? No! It's a Nommo!" argued one man.

"No! It's Antoa Nyamaa!"

"Wait, wait, my name is Aqua Maddas. I'm just a creature that lives in between the sea and this boat with my friend, the Listener," I introduced. "Call me Maddas for short."

"Mami Wata?" asked another.

"Never mind, it's not that important," I sighed. "What are your names?"

My question was followed by another long, awkward silence before one of the men started crying.

"I can't remember. The slave owners make us forget," the man sobbed.

"Well, take all the time you need. We get to places mostly by music and luck, so it might take us a little while to work out how to get to the Rio Grande," I said, trying to provide a calm, soothing tone to my voice whilst hoping that we could help our guests reach safety.

We were at sea for much longer than planned, and I neglected to tell our guests that time in the Listener's boat is on a slightly different track from human time. For instance, one day can equal a human year sometimes. I naively hoped that slavery would have ended by the time we had delivered our guests to the Rio Grande.

It also meant that we could spend some time helping our guests to heal a little bit by playing soothing music and introducing them to a pod of bottlenose dolphins that visited our boat. A docile nurse shark also joined us for a little bit, happy to be petted, and generously glad to share the location of the nutritious shellfish that it was hunting.

After letting our guests unwind with the restorative power of the Caribbean Sea and its wildlife, they slowly regained their spirits and a sense of their identities. They re-acquainted themselves with their tribal tattoos, their original languages, and their sense of purpose.

"My name is Ododo," smiled one of the women. "I am Yoruba."

"Bekoe," a young man said proudly. "It means I have come to fight."

"Esi," smiled another woman. "Bekoe and I are Ashanti."

"Ukeme," introduced the second man. "Means 'strength' in Ibibio."

"Azuka," the third man announced. "It means 'confidence' in Igbo."

"I still cannot remember," sighed the fourth man as he felt the scars on his arms. "I feel like I will never remember."

"I hope that when we get you to the river, it will help your memory. It's OK to have a fresh start and call yourself by a new name though if you want to?" I suggested.

We arrived at the mouth of the Rio Grande river whilst listening to the 'Music of the Maroons', but we switched off the record player the closer we came to land. As the sun was setting, we could see patrolling soldiers disappearing from their stations on the coast. Once it was nightfall, we were able to slip past the gazes of those who could re-capture our guests.

"We will take you up the river as far as we can," I declared.

The Listener frowned at me, unsure if the boat was suitable to carry us upstream and worried about us getting captured ourselves.

"Don't you have some magical powers that can help us, Maddas?" Ododo asked.

"A Nommo can control the flow of river water? Is that correct?" the unnamed man asked.

"I can cause storms, but I've never tried moving a river," I worried.

"I'm sure you can do it!" Azuka cheered confidently.

"Um...sure" I grinned nervously as the Listener shook his head at me.

That night, our little boat followed the sounds of chanting up the Rio Grande. After the first couple of bends, the river began to get narrower and tougher to navigate. We also noticed crocodiles eyeing us from the water. The Listener folded his arms and shook his head even more determinedly.

Amidst the sound of our passengers debating on what to do next, I noticed that the chanting was not coming from the Listener's record player. It was pouring from the Rio Grande river water itself. I dipped my webbed hands into the water, feeling as though a woman's voice was reaching me through the carried vibrations.

"Aqua Maddas, join hands with me. Together we can move the river to get these people to safety," the voice ordered, but in a calm, soothing tone.

"You know my name?!" I gasped, before regaining composure. "I've never done this before. I will try my best. Who are you?"

"Get these people to safety, and then I will reveal myself when you get here," the voice stated.

"OK, so a mysterious voice from the water will help me to carry you up to the mountains to safety, hopefully. Please arm yourself with some of my spears," I deliberated, gifting our guests with the collection of my make-shift spears.

I placed my hands back into the water, acutely aware of how close a crocodile was to our boat. Energised by the power flowing from the chanting as it reached me through the water, and using all the energy from the rage I felt at the suffering experienced by our six rescuees; we were able to change the flow of the river. Water leaving the mouth of the Rio Grande turned back on itself instead of joining the sea. A tide took our boat as if it were being carried by a giant 'hand' of water and lifted us, over the rocky rapids and the narrow passageways.

The river water carried us at such a speed; any wandering soldiers who spotted us were often too confused to pose a threat. Torrents of water from the wave shot towards anyone that tried to chase us. A few enemies were defeated by some impressively accurate spear throws from our guests.

By the time we had reached the small town where the voice had originated, I had become completely exhausted. As the boat drifted towards the settlement, I stumbled and fell unconscious on the deck.

I woke up to find our boat moored up onto a riverbank, surrounded by people armed with guns and spears. Some of the spears were ones I had gifted, which I found to be more flattering than intimidating in all honesty. Amongst the commotion, I heard the voice of the woman I had teamed up with to move the river. She strode out from the river water and met me face-to-face. A white cloth wrapped her short, curly black hair. Armed with a gun and spear, she also carried an intense yet kind gaze in her dark brown eyes.

"I am Queen Nanny," she introduced whilst shaking my hand and inspecting my webbed fingers.

"Thank you for moving the river with me, Queen Nanny. I had no idea that we could do that," I gasped with awe.

"I have my strengths and secrets," she grinned. "As do you. You have more powers than you think."

"Not enough, though. I am sorry I could only help save six people. I wish I could do more," I sighed sadly.

"This is not your fight, Aqua Maddas. You have your path," Nanny replied wisely. "The six you have brought here will live with us in the Mountains, and we will fight the slave owners.

We will fight them with everything we have. I see that one day, we will win. We will win a better future."

"Apart from patrolling the Atlantic for slave boat survivors, I'm not sure what else I can do to help," I murmured.

"I see many things of the future, Maddas. As I said, this is not your fight. But you can help us in little ways. If you see injustice happening to others due to the colour of their skin, speak up against it. Never stay quiet and passive, for this is not the way of the Maroons. Keep our story alive when history may want to silence our tales."

We ate generous amounts of deliciously spiced food and drank fresh, tasty river water before happily joining the Maroons during a celebratory dance. As usual, my large, webbed feet and clumsy body provided much entertainment as I tripped myself up whilst attempting to skip and jump.

Eventually, the Listener and I needed to get back to the ocean. After enjoying our time with Nanny and her ever-growing family, we embraced our previous guests warmly, and I shed briny tears on having to part with our lovely new friends. I thanked them from the bottom of my heart for trusting me.

"I know what my new name will be," the unnamed man decided, catching me before we left the town.

"Oh, that's great!" I cheered.

"I will call myself Nommo, like you," he grinned.

"Oh...yes. That is perfect," I smiled awkwardly before hugging him.

"Now please keep that name safe!" I called out to him as the Rio Grande river pushed us back to sea with a little bit of help from the mystical Queen Nanny."

"So, Fergus, before you tell Agwe to go back to where he came from, remember slave traders *took* his ancestors *from* Africa. The magical Nanny that I met was the leader of one group of Maroons. The Maroons were a group of slaves that escaped the slave owners and fought against them," Maddas concluded, surprised that their story had held Fergus's attention.

Fergus stared blankly at Patient Seven and then gazed at Agwe who had appeared suddenly.

"Time for your medication, Fergus," Agwe sighed. Maddas noticed that Agwe's mood had changed dramatically in the last hour or so.

"Thank you, Agwe. I'm so sorry for how I am," Fergus sobbed as he gently took his pills.

"Fergus is acting slightly differently," Maddas noticed, hoping that their story had changed the way Fergus was thinking.

"Oh, this man goes from an angry racist in the morning to guilty and ashamed in the evening. It's all part of his condition," Agwe replied glumly.

"Agwe, what's wrong?" Maddas asked. "You were so happy earlier. What's happened?"

"Well, Maddas. Guess who didn't get paid today?" Agwe grumbled.

"That's terrible, I'm sorry," Patient Seven exclaimed, trying to be soothing despite rage creeping back into their mind.

"It's not the first time for me, and the same goes for other Nurses who look like me," he sighed. "My daughter won't get her birthday present this weekend after all."

"I'm sorry, Agwe. You obviously love your daughter very much though, and honestly that's the best gift a parent can give their child," Maddas tried.

"I'm sure it is," Agwe murmured. "But that's not the point though is it."

Duryonyon

Patient Seven slumped on a sofa in the communal area after retrieving a sketch pad from their room. They decided to do some doodling whilst casually watching the weekday Nurses swapping shifts with unfamiliar faces. The weekend staff glumly readied themselves for a possibly eventful couple of days as Maddas channelled feelings of inner rage into sketching unrecognisable shapes.

Abruptly, a man came to sit beside Maddas on the sofa. He seemed distraught and fidgety as he scratched at his little mane of curly, grey-brown hair.

"I'm terrified, friend," the man began in a nervous, hurried voice.

"What's wrong?" Maddas asked, placing the sketch pad to the side.

"There's a man here - he won't stop until he gets what he wants. He wants to kill me," he explained, holding his distressed head in his hands.

"My name is Maddas. Can I ask your name?" Patient Seven cut in, trying to change the subject.

"Jeff," the man winced.

"OK Jeff," Maddas nodded, looking around them furtively, trying to catch sight of any perpetrator. "Look, you're safe with me. I won't let anyone hurt you, I promise," Maddas affirmed in an assertive, protective tone.

"Do you understand what I'm talking about?" Jeff asked intensely.

"Yes, as a matter of fact, I do," Maddas nodded. "I remember a time when we picked up someone in our boat who seemed steadfast in wanting to murder us."

"It happened just after I had swum alongside a gargantuan basking shark as it drifted slowly near the surface of the Celtic sea. Imagine swimming next to a gigantic bus with an enormous open mouth. I was relieved to find out that it was not interested in eating me but instead gorged on plankton blooms that fuzzed the visibility of our surroundings. I remember that it looked at me with a confused expression as I mimicked its open mouth in a crude attempt to bond with it. As it wearily swam away from me, I took that as my cue to get back to the Listener's boat.

After I clambered back to the deck, I suddenly started to dance wildly to the sound of Cornish chant music from the Listener's record player. I took a slightly surprised Listener by his fluffy hands and made him sway with me clumsily. We were so distracted by our dancing; we failed to notice the stranger that had appeared in our boat.

"Woah, hello! Can we help you in some way?" I greeted, suppressing my initial shock.

Our new companion had wrinkled, grey-blue skin and long, dark green hair intermixed with seaweed. He stared at us intensely with his cold, lifeless eyes as algae-blighted rags clung loosely to his lean body. His gaze and threatening grin suggested that he was not in search of friendship. He scanned our boat and frowned with confusion at the record player and the cardboard box of never-ending vinyl records.

He suddenly pushed the Listener out of the way, sending him ricocheting to the wooden deck before attempting to grasp the record player. His mission seemed to be to take control of our boat. The Listener tried to pull him away from the record player, but the attacker threw him to the other end of the cabin cruiser.

I then reacted, putting myself in between the enemy and the controls, and received a punch to the face from his cold, bony knuckles. Although barnacle shells decorated his sharp fist, I was that glad my face was harsh and scaly and that it had caused some amount of pain to the attacker's fist.

The man recovered quickly and tried to push me away from the record player.

"You're both going to die!" the man screeched at a terrifying volume. "This is my boat now!"

He kicked my torso with his impressively agile legs, and rigid, calloused feet. His long, jagged toenails rivalled my sharp claws. I lost my balance and ended up falling over, becoming stuck in place with my back spikes skewered to the wooden deck.

The man pulled out a small dagger from a hidden sheath underneath his ragged shirt and lunged towards me, attempting to stab me in the face as I lay on the ground. I protected myself just in time with my thick, scaly arms and elbow spikes, and then swiftly used my back legs and webbed feet to powerfully push-kick him away from me.

I leapt up into a fight-ready stance, and with some help from the fluctuant ocean, I used the tidal momentum to torpedo myself into the attacker. I grabbed him and pinned him to the deck, using my left foot to clamp down on his knife-wielding hand. With some force, I had him release the knife. The Listener grabbed it and threw it overboard to be swallowed by the sea.

"No!" he cried, attempting to punch and kick me again.

"You cannot have this boat," I snarled, baring my sharp teeth.

"I need it more than you, whatever you are?! Sea Monster!" the man cried.

"Takes one to know one," I retorted. "What on Earth are you?"

"I am the Duryonyon," he replied. "I need to take your boat and use it to save my family from a sinking ship!"

"You should have just told us in the first place!" I growled. "We could have helped you faster if you hadn't attacked us!"

"How does this weird boat even work?" he grumbled as I helped him up from the deck.

"Via record player and magic of course," I explained. "But, in this case, we can make an exception and steer it. Can't we?"

The Listener stood with arms crossed, seeming disgruntled about the plan to help the frightening-looking man and steer the ship without a fantastic soundtrack. He eventually agreed with a sigh after I had stared at him with my intense, unblinking opal-blue eyes.

"Keep playing the chants of Kernow, it will help," the man requested, sitting on the deck in a more subdued manner.

We half-followed the music and the Duryonyon's directions. On our journey, I attempted to understand more about this determined being.

"Duryonyon means 'survivor' in Cornish," he explained. "My family and friends were taken from the coast of Cornwall by pirates and put in shackles. The pirates were going to sell us as slaves far away from home."

"That's awful," I replied, trying to empathise. "I was captured by a pirate once who put me in a cage. It was a terrifying experience. You escaped, though?"

"The ship hit a rock and began to sink slowly. As our captors became distracted, I was able to slip out of my chains. I fought hard and attacked the pirates with the crab-hunting knife hidden underneath my vest. The knife that you threw into the ocean, sea monster," he snarled at me.

"I apologise for nothing. You tried to stab me in the face," I grumbled. "Anyway, continue your story, Duryonyon."

"I tried to unchain as many people as I could. There were no escape boats on the ship, so I dived into the ocean and swam until exhaustion, searching for a boat to help me."

123

"Wow, you are one tough soul," I nodded, both impressed and still quite scared of our new friend.

The boat arrived at the rocky outcrop where the sinking ship was supposed to be. The Listener scratched his head of matted black hair, and I mumbled to myself with confusion at the lack of ship.

"I can dive down underwater to see if there are any survivors. You never know," I suggested.

The Listener grasped my arm and frowned at me angrily. I pulled a spike from my back and gave it to him for protection.

"If you take our boat, I will find you," I glowered at the Duryonyon. Somehow, he did not seem as much of a threat as earlier. The way he sat and looked down at the deck made him seem smaller than before.

Taking care to avoid the rocks, I dived into the ocean and caught sight of the remains of a shipwreck. I took a closer look and saw that the wreck was a much older carcass than expected. Most of the wood had become rotten, with metal parts rusted over and more home to sea life than humans. Small wrasses and octopuses swam about the vegetation that had swallowed most of the boat. Lobsters crawled around remnants of the deck as I searched for any signs of humans. All I could find were a couple of bones and perhaps half of a skull.

With a confused and heavy heart, I prepared myself to swim to the surface to inform the Duryonyon of the bad news. As I slowly swam upwards, I noticed that around the shipwreck were the remains of many other boats. Most of them were small boats, and they looked younger than the main wreckage. Shocked and even more confused, I left the ocean and was relieved to find that our cabin cruiser was still there and intact.

"Um, how long were you swimming for, Duryonyon?" I asked with a soft tone to my voice as I sat down next to our guest.

"I don't know. It seems like many lifetimes," the man sighed sadly.

"What would you have done with our boat if you had taken it from us?" I probed further.

"I would have taken it to the sinking ship, to find that the ship is no longer there. Then, I would have driven it into the rocks and then returned to swimming and searching for another boat again. Such is my existence. I am doomed to repeat this cycle of losing and taking," the man explained. "I am not just known as the Duryonyon. I am also known as Gorra Dhe-Ves. It means to 'take away'."

"Is there anything we can do to help you break out from this curse?" I tried.

"You've done it already," the man murmured, looking directly at me with a kinder gaze despite his cold, dead eyes. "You were strong enough to fight back, but you were even stronger in that you took the time to understand who I am and what my troubles are. Most people just want to focus on overfishing these oceans than care about my struggles."

"I mean, people would have taken the time to understand you if perhaps you hadn't threatened them or taken their boats," I reasoned.

"It is never an easy thing to ask for help, especially if you look like a monster," the man explained. "Sometimes it's easier to attack first and take from other poor souls than risk others attacking you. But thank you for listening to me and hearing my story. You're one of the good sea monsters."

I blushed in response, but it was challenging to see under my scaly blue-green skin.

"Keep my history alive, so that it may never repeat. No one will ever take the Cornish from their homes again. Otherwise, I will come back," the Duryonyon threatened.

"I will do my best," I smiled, watching with curiosity as the man stood up and prepared himself to jump back into the ocean.

"One day you will have the strength to face your own trauma as well," he spoke with great sincerity before diving.

He left our boat, but there was no sound of a splash. It seemed as though he just vanished into the threads of time, hopefully to the freedom of the afterlife."

"What I am trying to say to you, Jeff is yes. Yes, I have been in danger, and someone wanted to take everything important to me. But he did not take my kindness. I am sometimes more wary of others now, and I fight to keep what is special in my life. Others threatening me will not turn me into an unkind person though," Maddas concluded.

Jeff had been half-listening, which was more than enough for Patient Seven. He nodded respectfully.

"Maddas, do you mind if I hide in your room for a little bit?" Jeff asked.

Patient Seven debated with themselves for a little while before smiling warmly.

"If this will help you, sure," Maddas agreed before letting Jeff follow them to the corridor of the ward that took them to Maddas's room. They both arrived at the door marked '7'.

"You're welcome to hide next to my bed," Maddas gestured towards a mini fort built from books, newspapers and magazines that had been collected and hoarded from the communal area. "I can guard you against whoever is trying to kill you."

"Maddas, I need to tell you something," Jeff whispered, indicating for Maddas to come closer to him to hear what he wanted to say.

"What is it?" Maddas questioned, making sure to keep their distance.

"It's me," Jeff hissed.

"Huh?"

"The killer is me. I am the one who is trying to kill me. Isn't that funny?" Jeff guffawed. "I thought you'd enjoy a good plot twist, Maddas the Storyteller!"

"Um," Patient Seven replied with a frown.

"Perhaps I will kill you instead," Jeff grinned, snarling threateningly at Maddas.

"Get off my boat! I mean, get out of my room!" Maddas boomed, flaring their shoulders, and showing Jeff their sharp claws and teeth to intimidate him. "Leave!"

Jeff quickly scuttled out of the room, still chuckling to himself as he skipped down the corridor, looking for someone else to bother.

Maddas shut their door, making sure they had it locked at least several times. They slumped on their bed and sighed.

"Be careful who you let into your boat," they muttered to themselves, scratching their scaly forehead with their serrated claws. "It's these moments that make me feel grateful that I'm a monster."

Part 2: Transformations

Human-Ish

Patient Seven stood in the doorway of their dormitory room whilst involved in an intense conversation with a female Nurse.

"As I said, sometimes I'm happier being a monster, Shona," Maddas explained to her as calmly as they could. Shona showed a kind gaze through her hazelnut eyes and was trying her best to convince Maddas to take a small vanity kit.

"Self-care and making yourself look good and feel good is one of the first signs of recovery," she pressed, placing a plastic case with a comb, toothbrush, toothpaste, and soap into Maddas's webbed claws. "Please take this. It is for you."

"I'd rather you give this to someone else. Maybe someone else needs it more?" Patient Seven argued, attempting to give the case back to Shona. "No matter how hard I try, I will always be this."

Shona quickly gave the case back to Maddas and hurried away. Maddas sighed and took the kit with them back into their room where they hid behind a small mountain of books and magazines.

Later that day, Patient Seven spoke to Susan, the Therapist, about how they felt about their appearance.

"So, have you ever tried to change how you look?" Susan asked them.

"Yes, I have," Maddas began.

"After the violent encounter with the Duryonyon, the Listener and I had a fierce argument. Soon after we had said goodbye to our scary new friend, the Listener turned to me with his arms folded. It was difficult to see his expression underneath his overgrown black, curly mane. However, I could tell that he looked disgruntled. He frowned and stubbornly refused to play any more records.

"What's wrong?" I asked him, but I received the usual silence.

"Look, helping people and making friends can be a dangerous business. It's rough, just like the sea. But it's also beautiful and rewarding, again, just like the sea!" I yelled, waving my arms in an attempt to convince the Listener.

Still, the Listener folded his arms and frowned silently.

"What am I supposed to do? Do I spend my eternity with a silent hairy thing and just go where the music takes us? I want to be in charge of my destiny! I don't want to be a prisoner on an island or a boat! I want good conversation and human connection, not just music!"

Hairy silence was the reply.

"OK then, I will leave this boat. I am going to find the nearest available land and make myself as 'human-looking' as I can. I have made my body adapt to the sea, so I'm sure I can make it into something human-ish!"

The Listener shrugged and sighed a sad sigh. We drifted towards a small island with a rocky beach. There, I said a terse goodbye to the

Listener and his boat and watched him drift away from me. However, I had a feeling it would not be the last time I saw him.

I sat on the grey rocks, staring at the sea. From my vantage point, I saw various sized ships passing by. Some were carrying metal boxes of cargo, and some moved crowds of people. Thankfully, this time, the people were not in chains.

There, I sat cross-legged on that cold, windy beach for many days and nights, staring at my reflection in rock pools and focusing my mind on every human I had ever encountered. Each day, a part of my appearance changed. The cartilaginous horns on my head melted into my green hair, which then darkened in colour to become brown with a few aquamarine streaks. The spikes on my shoulders and back flattened and disappeared into my body. My scales transformed into clammy skin, or as skin-like as possible. My claws became non-webbed hands and feet with nails that could have benefited from a file.

My blue eyes stayed mostly the same, and I could not do anything about the slightly damp nature of my skin and hair. I also could not do much about my gills, although they were a lot more subtle and hidden by my new long hair.

Before I even summoned the courage to try out my new appearance on one of the passenger boats passing by, I knew I had to find some clothes. I scavenged for any discarded items around the rocky beach and searched the surrounding sea. Thankfully, I was still able to dive despite losing my foot-webs.

A part of me wished for some padded or protective clothes after being at the mercy of human weapons for many centuries. However, I had to make do with a slightly torn white shirt and some soggy, greenish-brown trousers. A part of me psychologically kicked myself at not asking Cortissos for one of his gowns so many years ago.

After becoming 'human-ish' and working out how to brush my hair with my hands, it was time to enter the human race. I had set my eyes on a passenger ship and timed my swim perfectly, grateful that I was still a fast and powerful swimmer. With no apprehension - just excitement at who I might meet, I found a ladder on the side of the ship and clambered aboard..."

"Wow, what a transformation," nodded Susan, the Therapist as she wrote notes on a pad as usual. "Did you get the vanity kit that the Nurses wanted to give to you by the way?"

"I'm going to give it away," Maddas decided.

Later that day, Maddas had taken the small, plastic vanity kit with them to the communal area. They searched around, hoping to find the right person to receive the gift. On seeing that Jeff was bothering a young, shy-looking boy, Maddas felt as though it was their duty to break up what could become a disastrous interaction for the young one.

After a closer look, Maddas realised that the boy resembled a seahorse in some ways. His face was long and thin and displayed wide, intelligent eyes that were magnified by glasses with thick lenses. He had tiny but sharp spines decorating the top of his head that also followed his backbone as well as protecting his shoulders and chest. His hands and feet were spiked, webbed claws, just like those that belonged to Maddas.

Cheerfully, Patient Seven gave the 'Seahorse Boy' the vanity kit. Startled by the sudden interaction with Maddas and possibly worn down by Jeff, the boy smiled at Maddas but immediately scuttled away to a corridor. He disappeared, most likely to the privacy of his dormitory room.

Yosef

Patient Seven sat in the Therapist's room, beginning another session with Susan. Maddas was transfixed by the art on the walls, especially one picture of a bright red starfish.

"Oh, how I miss the sea," Maddas sighed with a small sob.

"So, when you boarded the boat after turning yourself 'human-ish', who did you meet?" Susan asked Maddas, readying herself to write copious amounts of shorthand in a fresh notepad.

"When I first emerged after climbing aboard the passenger boat, I was met by groups of huddled people with confused, distraught expressions on their faces. After a few minutes, however, the people ignored my presence. My ragged clothes were not too dissimilar from the outfits worn by the passengers. The people on the boat looked starving, exhausted, and sick. Many people were crying. Small children were playing with wooden spinning toys whilst their parents watched over them, praying to something in the sky that they hoped would help them.

As I passed through the crowd, I let my ears gain familiarity with their language. There was the temptation to join a small gathering of people, introduce myself and hope for the best. However, it was one individual that caught my attention first. I remember seeing a young man all by himself, and I felt as though I needed to meet him.

He had his arms wrapped around his torso in a self-hug, and he was muttering to himself. His breathing was rapid and by the look of his pale cheeks and blue lips, not providing him with enough oxygen. His skin almost matched the blue-green hue of mine. He grasped at his curly, dark brown hair and gripped his forehead in an attempt to gain control of a mind that encased him in anguish.

"Hi there," I greeted him.

Initially, he ignored me and carried on muttering to himself.

"Hello, can you hear me?" I tried again with no success.

Instead of a third go, I sat beside him and tried to listen to what he was saying.

"It's all gone. We're all going to die. It's all gone. We're all going to die. We have to go. It's all gone..." the young man repeated to himself.

Other passengers passed him by, leaving some space between themselves and the suffering young man. My presence was not exactly helping as people kept even more distance between themselves and me. Perhaps I looked very sick to them.

"You are not going to die," I assured him with a matter of fact tone and a supportive pat on the shoulder. At that moment, I was relieved not to possess sharp claws.

"Are you real? You seem real. That pat felt real. I am not sure, though. Are you real?" he asked, glancing at me quickly in a bashful manner before covering his face with his hands.

"I am as real as I can be," I smiled, not quite knowing what to say or do next.

"Are you sick too?" he asked. "Your skin is blue."

"Oh, that's just… me," I grinned with a nervous shrug. "What's your name?"

"Yosef," he replied. "You?"

"Maddas," I smiled, holding out my recently transformed hand with pride. Yosef shook my hand cautiously.

"Can I ask, are you male or female?" he frowned.

I had not quite worked that one out. Moments of silence that felt like years followed Yosef's question as I tried to search for the best answer.

"Next question please," I answered quickly, with another nervous smile.

"OK," he replied flatly.

A couple of minutes passed, again that felt like aeons.

"You're still here," he commented.

"Is that OK? Do you want me to go?" I asked, bracing myself for rejection.

"Yes. Um, no. I mean, yes that is OK. No, I do not want you to go," Yosef clarified.

"Oh, that's good," I sighed with relief.

"Most people go. Most people avoid me. I am sick, and people say the devil has cursed me. Perhaps I am the devil. Am I the devil, Maddas?" he asked, his eyes met mine and revealed such pain and dehydration.

"I've been called a devil before as well," I mentioned. "I do not think that you are a devil, Yosef. You look thirsty. Do you want me to get you some water? I can find some for you."

"No. I will drink when I'm on land. If I have anything now, I will throw up," he winced, wrapping his arms around his stomach.

"Shall I stay sitting here?" I asked.

"Yes. But, in silence, though please," Yosef said quickly. "I'm too ill to talk. Also, I'm still not convinced that you're real."

"I'm real," I assured him. "Yes, let's sit and just be."

So, there we sat together for about an hour or so. I just stayed there with my hands resting on my lap in a meditative pose, guarding Yosef as he struggled mentally and physically. After a while, his breathing calmed down.

As we began to approach land, Yosef stood up suddenly and peered at his new homeland.

"I sold my lute to come here," he mentioned. "What if they refuse us?"

As the ship weaved its way through the River Thames, I remember being impressed at the beautiful and mighty buildings of London. Crowds of people gathered around where the vessel was attempting to dock. At first, I believed these people to be family and friends of those on the boat. However, the shouts and cries of the crowd seemed upset, bordering on aggressive. They were holding up signs with sprawl that I could not quite read. I did, however, hear a couple of words that I understood.

"No more refugees! Refugees go back home!" they bellowed.

"We sold everything to escape. We also spent money sent to us from our families here. People were trying to kill us. They're going to send us back. I can't go back; they will kill me. They will kill me, I can't go back," Yosef uttered, wrapping his arms around his torso, and rocking back and forth.

"It's going to be fine, I promise," I assured him, faking my confidence.

I leapt off the ship and dived into the Thames, immediately regretting the decision. To my mistake, I had found myself in the most unhygienic body of water that had ever existed. Drenched in mulch and letting my feet and hands regrow their webs and claws a little, I strode purposefully yet slightly clumsily up a muddy beach and climbed up to where the crowds were.

The people were so astonished to see a weird aquatic humanoid emerge from the Thames that they turned their attention away from the refugee ship. I did anything I could to distract them until the passengers were off the boat. For a fraction of a second, the crowd saw a few regrown spikes on my shoulders, my webbed claws, and my spiny forehead horns.

The refugees hurried off the ship as people became obsessed with trying to draw and photograph the 'Thames River Monster'. It was the least I could do to help the passengers get to safety and find new, hopefully, peaceful lives in the East End of London.

Eventually, I became claustrophobic from the crowd of people. On meditating for a few minutes, I summoned a thunderstorm with thick, grey-black clouds, heavy with rain and crackling lightning. Aggressive weather was enough to disperse my 'fan club' and provide me enough cover to 'de-monster' just in time to catch Yosef before he disappeared into the metropolitan jungle.

"What did you do? Who are you? Are you real?" Yosef cried, outstretching his arms briefly to gesture for a hug but then quickly wrapping them around himself protectively.

"I think I am real, but now I'm starting to question it," I joked, patting Yosef on his bony shoulder again.

"I will go now. I will work and get myself a new lute, or a guitar. Some kind of musical instrument. Will you come with me? I've heard this is an island of opportunity," he put forward.

'Why oh why did he have to say 'Island'?' I thought to myself, baring my teeth nervously out of habit. I looked towards the city full of humans, cars, and noise. I had wanted so much for an invitation to a world that was out of my reach for millennia. However, it was too overwhelming for me at that moment. The sea was still calling my name, pulling me back to its refreshing, healing embrace. I could not be a part of this new island, not just yet.

"Maybe I will join you later. Go! Go and enjoy your new life! I will try to find you again, Yosef," I smiled, mentally preparing myself to jump into the Thames again, change back into a monster and swim to the sea.

"OK. Bye Maddas," Yosef replied, still with the same flatness, but a brief inflexion betrayed some emotion. He took slow, cautious steps towards the commotion, sometimes patting sooty walls to steady himself.

I was elated to be accepted by humans, or at least, one human. But it meant risking my freedom on another island - one that could trap me again. Would I lose myself and have to live as a human-like creature forever?

Fortunately, a melody cut through the noise of the people, boats, and my thoughts. The Listener in his little musical boat had found his way back into my life again. I heard chaotic, energetic music beaming from his record player. I jumped aboard and gave my friend a tight, slightly painful hug. He replied with a small smile and patted my arm affectionately, gesturing towards the cover of the record playing.

"Clisma? Kl...azmer? Klezmer?" I muttered, trying to read the words on the album cover."

"Klezmer? What's that? I've never heard of it," the Therapist frowned. "Anyway, did you see Yosef again?"

"Klezmer is the traditional music of the Ashkenazi Jews," Maddas informed. "And yes, I did see Yosef again, but he had changed a lot in between the time he had arrived and when I decided it was *my* time...to arrive."

Patient Seven felt incredibly flattered at how transfixed Susan was regarding one of their most treasured memories.

Are you from the Sea?

"How do you mean, changed?" Susan, the Therapist, probed, either jotting down a couple of notes in her notebook or just doodling. It was not entirely clear.

"It took a lot of energy to summon storms and rain, so I rested in the Listener's boat for a while. We were well hidden amongst many other boats and ships in the docklands of the Thames," Maddas carried on.

"I had grown used to the odours, but I welcomed the smell of fresh rain, especially when it arrived through no effort on my part. As we were in London, we did not necessarily have to wait long for rain. However, building up the courage to enter the city and walk on land took me what I thought was only a couple of days.

I had utterly forgotten that time in the Listener's boat was different from human time, whilst I procrastinated. I tortured myself mentally about what could happen if I left the ocean for too long, how long my human-ish appearance would last and if I would be accepted at all by humanity.

My thoughts were interrupted by realising that the Listener was not playing any records. Amidst the gentle tapping of the rain, I heard an incredible sound that reached my ears not from the record player, but through the water that trickled down from cobbled streets and into the Thames. It was the melodic sound of a stringed instrument and beautiful, gentle vocals.

"OK, I have to follow this," I stated determinedly. The Listener gave me a thumbs up, which I understood was his way of wishing me good luck.

On land, my ears twitched, and my mind searched as I placed the palms of my hands in the rivers of rainwater gushing through the streets. I used the interconnectedness of the temporary waterways to work out the origin of the sound. The city had become an aquatic environment, and that was welcoming to me. Sometimes I rested in puddles as I strode through alleyways, taking time to process my new surroundings.

I had entered a red-brick world of pure, enchanting chaos. There were bold, elegant signs for shops, businesses and market stalls, all jostling for the attention of passers-by. Warm, inviting shopkeepers greeted me as they tried to sell me beautiful clothes, intricately made shoes and some of the most enticing food I had ever encountered.

I stood outside one clothes shop, inspecting a particular item in the window. It was a turquoise gown with slightly spiky-looking shoulders, and I thought I saw a label that read 'Cortissos'. Before the shopkeeper could register my interest, I ran away.

A part of me wished I had money, but because I was wearing ragged clothes and had bluish skin, a lot of traders looked at me with pity. I am not ashamed to say that I fell in love with a free beigel or two. The smell of warm bread and succulent salted meat overcame me and almost made me forget about the melody I was hearing.

I pressed on, shielding myself as crowds of people rushed through the narrow, corridor-like streets. Even though it was still pouring with rain, it did not stop people from laughing and cheering with each other underneath umbrellas. One kind person saw my wet hair and soggy clothes and gave me their umbrella without much thought. I was about to tell them 'no, I'm an aquatic creature and I relish the rain', but instead, I grinned sheepishly.

"Thank you so much you kind soul," I said to them, before trying to figure out how to manoeuvre the weird contraption against the wind.

The melody grew stronger as I travelled down a quiet, shadowy alleyway. There I found him, sitting on the pavement in front of a locked-up shop. He played a worn-out, rain-soaked guitar, and tried to sing with a sore, raspy throat. In front of him was a small hat with a couple of coins.

"Yosef?!" I cried out, eager to see his gaunt, weathered face again.

"Maddas?!" he croaked. "Just what I need - another hallucination on top of being homeless, penniless and it not stopping raining for months!"

"You're not hallucinating!" I grumbled. "Look, take this very real umbrella that I can't figure out how to use. I don't need it."

"Are you sure you don't need it? If you're real, you do look quite blue. You might be sicker than me."

"Honestly, it's just my normal colour. I can't change it," I sighed. "And I can't give you coins. I don't have them, and I can't work out how to get them. This umbrella is all I can give you. Perhaps I can get you a free beigel?"

"You know, I do like the rain in some weird way," Yosef admitted. "It takes ages to get dry again, but the streets are emptier, less crowded and chaotic. People attack me less during the rain. They are too concerned with trying to get dry than to attempt to take my guitar."

"I'm sorry that people attack you," I replied with a soothing voice. "You play excellently. I heard you from the river."

"I carry that far?" Yosef frowned.

"If you have special ears like I do, then yes," I grinned, slowly sitting myself down beside

Yosef on the pavement, and working out how to get comfortable on the cold, stony ground.

"What are you?" Yosef asked, his piercing brown eyes boring straight into my soul with his stare. "I remember that I saw you on the ship that brought us. Protestors almost stopped us from coming to London. Suddenly you turned up, and we were all let in."

"Well, I hope you can call me a friend?" I tried.

"You're a very odd person. But I don't have many friends. People always tell me I am too odd. Too mad. So yes, I hope I can call you a friend?"

We shook hands, but gently. Yosef's delicate hands were so bony due to malnutrition, but they still had a particular strength from his music. I had an insecurity that my hands would turn back into claws and slice his soft skin at any second.

"You know, when I first got this guitar," Yosef began, with a slight blush underneath his ghostly-pale skin. "Apart from playing my usual folk songs, I first wrote a song about you."

"You...what?" I gasped in disbelief.

"Can I sing it?"

"OK...yeah. Yes, sure," I spluttered, trying to remain calm and collected whilst filling with utter joy.

"It's not quite finished," he muttered bashfully, before beginning to strum powerfully.

"Who are you? Are you from the sea?

Somehow you, you can see me.

You sat beside me and calmed me down.

You let me in, I didn't drown.

You brought a storm,

Just what we need,

From being hunted down.

We were freed.

Oh, will I ever see you again?

Sat next to me?

That 'who are you'?

Who is from the sea?"

Tears emerged from my eyes. It was the only song about me that didn't feature the words 'devil', 'demon' or 'monster'. I felt 'seen' for the first time in my life. I wanted so much to hold him, kiss him, give him anything he wanted, but I breathed deeply and controlled myself. The last thing I wanted to do was scare him away.

"That was wonderful," I muttered softly before chirping loudly. "And, I noticed something, Yosef. More people gave you coins during that song!"

"Oh, excellent," Yosef grinned before coughing forcefully and rasping "But, what do you honestly think though?"

Perhaps I had controlled my emotions so much that Yosef mistook me for having none.

"It was...brilliant," I gasped, holding back more tears. "Yosef, more people need to hear your music!"

"Oh, I don't know about that," he smiled bashfully, with a little more colour added to his chiselled cheekbones.

"I want your singing to be on a record that I can listen to on my boat!" I cried. "I want the Listener to be able to play it, and always be able to take me to you."

Yosef reached for my hand and held it. His fingers felt like little ice cubes, and he wasn't taken aback by my clamminess. I hoped that our physical contact would provide him with even just a little bit of warmth.

"I get...stage fright though," he shuddered, almost shaking himself into a panic.

"But you're performing in front of a lot of people already by singing in the streets," I argued. "Plus, I will be there to help you. I can cheer you on if you get nervous. I want to see how people make records anyway. Call it curiosity..."

"Well, there is Levy's on Whitechapel High Street," he piped up. "I've always wanted to go there. But I need to build my confidence in my songs. Perhaps I should play at some music bars first?"

"Yes!" I agreed enthusiastically.

"But what if people boo me?" Yosef worried.

"If they do, I'll sort them out," I winked. "You've got me now. Consider yourself a turtle - I will be your shell."

"That could be a good song lyric. Although not too many people want to hear songs about turtles," Yosef mumbled to himself.

"These people sound awful," I chuckled, relishing laughing together with Yosef.

So, that is just what we did. We turned up at music bars, both nervous wrecks. However, I held my calm and stood stubbornly in the audience, letting other people become aware that I was with Yosef, supporting him.

It wasn't easy for me at first. Being there for my good friend meant going inside little, cave-like buildings. When it stopped raining for a while, I missed the feel of cold water on my skin. Sometimes I felt too far away from the Listener's boat, the river, and the sea. However, for Yosef, it was worth it.

At first, Yosef was nervous and jittery. After battling his stage-fright, he eventually moved people with his enchanting music. The more he played his songs - many of which I found difficult to understand but were seemingly very popular with the crowds, the more confident he became.

More and more people learnt of his name and appreciated his music. Sometimes I would stand in the shadows at the back of jam-packed rooms, whispering in peoples' ears about him being one of the most talented musicians in the world. Sometimes I would dance uncontrollably to the energetic sounds of the folk songs he played, taking advantage of having small, non-webbed feet. Yosef was so gifted that I and an ever-growing entourage of fans pushed him to put his music onto a record, finally.

I remember a time when Yosef's music was all I could hear. After him singing in bars and then recording an album, I was able to listen to his melodies on the boat with the Listener. He nodded his head approvingly after hearing one of Yosef's albums, 'Yiddish Kiddush'. A nod from the Listener was probably the most important and only measure of real success for a musician, in my opinion.

Crucially, Yosef was able to make himself a decent living. The last few times I saw him, we were walking through The Regent's Park. It was sometimes challenging to keep a conversation as passers-by would interrupt us and pressure Yosef into giving them autographs.

There was always the temptation to jump into the lake and get some much-needed hydration when the claustrophobic crowds were too overwhelming. It had been so long since I had swum in the ocean. I yearned for it, but I needed Yosef's company more. The lake would have to do.

"What on earth are you doing in the lake?!" he yelled at me, scratching his stylishly oiled hairstyle.

"Sorry," I grinned awkwardly as I climbed out of the lake, apologising to all the ducks I had disturbed.

When the crowds moved on, I decided to share some of my feelings of insecurity.

"Look, Yosef, I understand if you do not need me anymore. You probably don't want to spend time with a weirdo such as myself," I probed - sensing that Yosef had hundreds of things on his mind apart from me.

"Maddas, you were there for me at my lowest times," Yosef gasped, stroking my arm. "And you're not that weird. I mean, clean water isn't cheap here. I also used to bathe in the lakes a lot. Which reminds me, I own a flat now, Maddas."

"Oh, that's great. Congratulations!"

"It has a bath and everything..." he winked suggestively.

"OK," I nodded like the confused, naive person that I was.

"I'm saying that I'd like you to come to visit me at my flat," he smiled with another, more obvious wink.

"OK," I nodded. "I'd like to show you the magic music boat I live on too."

"I'd like that," he blushed.

We embraced tightly. Yosef whispered, "Let's meet here this Friday," before skipping away in his energetic, animated manner. It was fantastic to see how eating well really improved his bounce.

As soon as it dawned on me about what Yosef was hinting at, I immediately jumped back in the lake and swam some backstroke. I needed the cold water on my skin to think straight ever again."

Can You Stop the War?

"So, did you go through with visiting Yosef's flat?" asked the Therapist, enraptured in Patient Seven's story. They were so engrossed that it seemed they had forgotten to visit another patient.

"The next, and unfortunately the last time I saw Yosef - nothing went to plan," Maddas sighed sadly, mopping up tears from their scaly cheeks with a fresh stack of tissues.

"After my little swim in Regent's Park lake, I ran back to the Listener's boat. There, I danced and sang as the Listener played Yosef's compilation album, 'Putz Poetry'. My heart almost exploded whenever I heard the song that Yosef had written for me. It even appeared in the Listener's steadily populating 'Aqua Maddas' album after many, many songs about me being a Sea Devil. It was refreshing to hear some affection for once.

"Oh, what do I do, though?" I panicked, waving my arms at the Listener. "He wants me to visit his place. He said it seductively, I think. What should I do? How do I do it? What am I supposed to have? Do I need to change myself again?"

The Listener stroked their copious facial hair, thinking about my predicament for a couple of minutes before shrugging and looking for the next album to play. His eyes looked suddenly startled at the content of the records. I remember him gesturing to me that I needed to go and find Yosef.

I had again forgotten that time on the Listener's boat was different from human time. Still, once I had collected myself and had moulded some possibly useful private parts, I ran as fast as my clumsy human-ish feet could carry me. Even with the luxury of some well-made shoes gifted from Yosef, I wasn't fast enough to beat time.

And yes, I did see Yosef again at Regent's Park. But it was not the Friday he wanted. He looked completely different. He had grown much older and proudly displayed a full, bushy beard. He also appeared to be dressed in a uniform.

"Yosef?" I cried, waving a hand in front of his face.

"Maddas?!" he yelled. His face became purplish-red with outrage.

"Sorry for being so late," I murmured, feeling ashamed.

"Late?! It's been three years!" he cried. "When I didn't see you, it made me think that you were all in my head. You are just a hallucination, aren't you? Do not tell me otherwise! You're not real!"

"No, I'm just *terrible* at time-keeping," I winced.

"Every Friday I came to this park. I hoped to see you again. Now I see you, I still do not trust that you are real," he sighed. "But I will not be at this park again from tomorrow. I must leave to fight in the war."

"War?!" I cried.

"Yes. Surely even the most stupid hallucination should know about the war?!" Yosef shouted. "This country gave me safety. Now, I must fight for *its* safety."

"Fight? You?" I questioned in disbelief.

"Yes, me!" he snarled. "It's not like I have a choice. But still, I must serve."

"What kind of fighting?"

"I don't know yet. I must board a warship tomorrow and follow orders, I guess."

"But you might die," I shuddered.

"There is a strong possibility that I will die."

"You are so different from the man I met on the boat. You are even more different from the guitarist in the street, and the musician who wrote 'Meshuggeneh Melodies'," I exclaimed, trying to hold back from sobbing.

"Yes, I am different. Do you know why? Because you turn up in my life after a gap of many years!" he yelled. "Because my brain is faulty. I shouldn't even be allowed in the army, but still."

"Is there anything I can say or do to stop you from going?"

"Can you stop the war?" he retorted.

"I don't know, I've never tried."

"That was sarcasm," Yosef growled. "There's nothing you can do. I am sorry, Maddas, but I must do this. If somehow you are real, then our friendship must come to an end."

It was not the subject of war or death that hit me. It was the word 'end'. It ricocheted through my body like an uncontrolled bullet, and it awakened the monstrous creature that I had locked away for so long. First, the spikes on my back and shoulders re-appeared. They burst out from my slimy skin and ripped through my ragged shirt. My bluish skin revealed green-blue scales, and the gills on my neck became more apparent.

"Maddas? What's happening?" Yosef gasped, almost collapsing on the ground in shock.

My plan, I thought, had worked. I was hoping to scare Yosef so much that he would faint and forget all about boarding a warship and hopefully avoid a violent death. Instead, he collected himself and started to run away from me, backwards, after almost falling.

The spiky horns reappearing on my head suddenly became embedded within a mane of long, stretchy, violet-coloured tentacles. They burst forward from my face, grabbing Yosef, before reeling him back towards me.

The pain of saying goodbye, and the extreme wish to not let him leave my life turned me into more of a monster than I had ever been before. Even worse, I became aware that I was acting like the grasping vines of my original cursed Island. I had become 'The Grip' and had transformed into the Island of the Fallen personified, trying to keep Yosef from being free to choose his destiny. However, Yosef managed to punch and kick his way out of my tentacled clutch. I remember him looking at me with an expression that revealed a mix of fear and disgust.

"I'm glad I learnt a bit of boxing," he uttered to himself, before pushing me and my tentacle hair away from him forcefully. He sprinted away from me, and out of my life, forever."

"Oh, that's so sad," the Therapist swooned.

"I know," Maddas sighed.

"I remember crawling back to the boat. The Listener was also startled to see my new tentacle mane, where my human-ish hair used to be."

Switch Off

"I think it is a positive thing that you were able to recognise your destructive behaviour at a time of intense pain and grief," the Therapist smiled, offering Patient Seven a glass of water and some more tissues. "It's tough losing someone that you love very much and not become toxic in some way."

"Oh, but I was toxic for a little while," Maddas sighed before crying into what seemed to be a facemask of soggy tissues.

"It didn't matter how many storms I summoned; warships full of soldiers still set sail in the direction of carnage. It did not matter how much I meditated, nothing stopped submarines and U-boats from firing at each other and other ships, bringing watery graves to millions of people worldwide. It did not matter how many thick clouds I created, aircrafts passed over the sea, sometimes killing people, falling out of the sky and into the cold embrace of an unforgiving ocean.

During that time, I tried to block out the sounds of humans screaming - their prayers and howls often reached me through the ocean. When I had spent time in London with Yosef, he had introduced me to various delicious, mind-altering drinks - my favourite being vodka. It took a lot of that drink to silence the constant awareness of humanity in tatters but dulling my senses with spirits was an unhealthy coping mechanism for me for a while.

However, my personality started to match my monstrous appearance. Every song played by the Listener on the boat was a cry for help in some way. Even the more optimistic songs like 'Keep the Home Fires Burning' brought me intense emotional pain. I lashed out at the Listener as he sat there and did what he did best - to Listen. After every unsuccessful attempt at trying to stop battles at sea, I would retreat to the boat to growl and swear.

For a while, the fighting stopped, only to return years later. I did what I could, but I could not stop the cruelty, the pain, and the extinguishing of millions more human souls. The entire world had become as dangerous and as toxic as the Island of the Fallen.

Even though the Listener was still listening, there came a time when my presence on the boat caused him to shrivel up and become afraid. He avoided my gaze and stayed close to his record player. I realised that there were only so many times he could listen before he would either disappear from my life or kick me off the boat again. Also, I had reached my limits after trying to help humanity whilst still recovering from losing Yosef.

"I think I need to pause my relationship with humanity for a little while," I decided. "I'm sorry for being toxic. I am sorry for what I have become. Perhaps it is time for me to switch off the music. I will leave you in peace for now. Hopefully, I can find my tranquillity."

The Listener patted me on the shoulder before I took a deep breath, steadied myself, and dived into the ocean.

"Hang on, are you saying you were present during both world wars?" the Therapist frowned, gesturing towards a ward Nurse passing by the room.

"World War One and half of World War Two. I felt crushed by guilt, but I had to leave humanity to its own devices. Otherwise, I would have become drowned by human suffering at that time."

"I dived down into the ocean, seeing how deep I could go. As I swam, I adapted myself to survive in a world of heavy darkness. My ear canals widened, adjusting to the pressure.

When the sunlight became nothing but a murky blue, and then afterwards, just a memory, my eyes became enhanced with more rod cells so that I could see a little bit, although I became more accustomed to sensing through vibrations. Every cell in my body evolved and became more flexible to cope with the squeeze of the ocean.

Whatever lungs I had; they became no more. My spines became softer, and my turquoise skin metamorphosed into a more translucent appearance. Even though my organs became slightly visible, my bones strengthened themselves.

On reaching the bottom of the ocean, my body became larger. My wide eyes bulged from my face to 'see' both in front and above me. I had no idea what I had become in this quiet isolation, but it was what I needed to be at that time. There was a solemn calm from being a simple organism, walking through the deepest part of the world, just sensing and existing.

I passed through desolate deserts, beside the skeletons of whales and sometimes humans in shipwrecks. I strode through magnificent valleys and past mesmerising hydrothermal vents.

A school of bright lanternfish followed me for a while and dazzled me with their bioluminescence. Inspired by their beauty, I experimented with my skin. I let my soft scales develop bioluminescence themselves and enjoyed becoming a creature that glowed green.

Gulper eels gawped at me. They were either impressed at how I looked or perhaps that was just how their faces were.

It is unclear to me how long I spent at the bottom of the ocean. I went for ages without talking to a soul. My only company would be the weird animals if I could see them at all. The most exciting encounter I experienced was with a curious giant squid that travelled with me for some time before becoming bored and swimming away.

I was alone, and I felt empty, but also content. I needed that void so that I could process the agony I felt after losing someone who really 'saw' me. Though Yosef did not see the completely 'real' me, they accepted the complexity of who I was deep inside, beneath whatever veneer I had at the time.

I did not want to hear music for a long time because no music could ever lift my soul like that song he sang for me. No tune could energise or soothe me, especially in a world which invested in new, scary machines to destroy itself.

Even though I was so far away from the world of humans, I still felt the vibrations from the ships thudding on the ocean floor and the dropping of bombs.

Then one day, I walked uphill towards a nearby landmass and let myself float slowly back to the surface. My body re-adjusted gently, gained its blue-green colour, lost its bioluminescence, and re-formed its lungs. My eyes shrank back to normal, as did the rest of my body, and I let the sea carry me to wherever next.

I remember drifting my way onto a beach surrounded by a forest. As I lay there, my ears gradually found the sounds of the sea lightly patting the sand, seabirds calling to each other and the faint chirping of sparrows in the forest nearby. The harmony of the ocean mixed with the birdsong was the first 'music' I had heard for years, but it was the best thing for me to hear. It was a call to enjoy the here and now, rather than to wallow in the past."

"Ah, so that's why you like to sit in the yard and listen to the birds?" Susan asked.

"Well, I've got to do something to help me survive these awful pills they're giving me," Patient Seven grumbled. "I think I will go and sit outside now. I feel as though I have opened up a lot today."

"I understand that this has been difficult. Thank you for your trust," Susan smiled.

"Thank you for being a good listener," Maddas uttered before striding with their heavy, webbed feet towards the yard.

Breathing deeply and appreciating the fresh air, Maddas slumped down on a wooden bench and let out a long sigh. The breeze was refreshing, and tiny flecks of rain added a thin, watery glitter to Patient Seven's greenish-blue face.

The Seahorse Boy from earlier stepped silently into the garden. He closed the ward door as gently as the pattering rain and cautiously sat down next to the spiky Maddas. He consciously left a little bit of space in between them both. A slight hiss from the boy's headphones punctuated the quiet and faint birdsong amidst the raindrops.

"Fancy a Listen?" they offered, handing their headphones to Patient Seven.

Flightsong

Maddas exhaled slowly with a sense of release at hearing music again from the Seahorse Boy's headphones. It reminded them of their time on the Listener's boat, and of how beautiful the world can be when accompanied by the right melodies.

"Thank you, I'm Maddas," Patient Seven introduced, holding out a claw to the Seahorse Boy.

"I'm Viktor," he replied quietly. "You know, you're brave to sit with your back to the door."

"You're brave to lend your headphones to someone who lives and breathes for music but hasn't heard it in days," Maddas retorted, still bathing in the warm glow of beautiful sounds from the headphones. "I guess we're both risk-takers."

"There's a man in there who wants to kill me. They mentioned that they're planning to kill you too," Viktor warned.

"With this medication, they're giving me, it feels like a lot of people are trying to kill me right now," Maddas laughed in a slightly maniacal way.

"Don't take it then. Flush it down the toilet, out to sea," Viktor smiled with a little tune to his voice.

"Haha, it seems we're very alike," Maddas nodded with a wink.

"Also, Alice is going to try to escape today," Viktor whispered.

"Alice? The Dawn Drawer?"

"Yes. Did you know that Alice can secretly turn into a bird? She's not eaten for ages so that she can be light enough to fly. Any moment now, Alice is going to jump on the tennis table and fly away from this place, to safety," he sighed admiringly, gazing back at the window of the complex to glance at the mysterious Alice.

She was sitting peacefully in the communal space, applying eyeliner in between her sketching.

"Oh right, I didn't realise she could do that," Maddas replied, feeling impressed.

"I wish people like us had wings and could fly," Viktor dreamed. "It would be nice to escape."

"People like us?"

"Ocean people," he clarified.

"Thing is, I know that I can escape easily. I have many tricks. But it is not my preferred option," Maddas stated.

"Oooh, are you going to cause a flood?" Viktor piped up excitedly. "Let me know when you're going to do it. I'll help! I've wanted to flood this place ever since I got here."

"Hmm, maybe," Maddas thought, stroking their scaly chin. "For me, I prefer erosion. The ocean can be so many different things, just like me. Gentle, healing, threatening, dangerous, passive, or aggressive. It's difficult to know which one to be at any given time."

"It's all too easy to choose passive aggression," Viktor sniggered.

"Funnily enough, I used to know someone like Alice. She was another being who could fly," Maddas began.

"After my time in the deep sea, she was one of the few people in this world who reached out to me first. As I lay on a beach, trying to enjoy the peace of birdsong for a little while longer, a ringing sound pierced through the calm.

I sat up suddenly, trying to work out what I was hearing. It seemed to be coming from the sea. That or the rising tides were carrying the sound to me. I slid back into the ocean and swam with a steady, purposeful backstroke, following the shrill call. It led me to an isolated cave, carved by the sea into the side of a vertical cliff. I peered upwards to try to see the peak of the ridge, but clouds hid the summit.

On exploring the cave, I found it led to a beautiful, secluded beach. No humans could reach it without a boat, which was good for me, at least for a while. There, at the back wall of the cave was a wooden, wall-mounted phone. It had a receiver, but no dial or keypad. It continued to ring, teasing my curiosity. I cautiously picked up the receiver.

"Hello?" I spoke slowly.

"Is that the Sea Monster, Aqua Maddas?" replied a joyful female voice.

"...Yes," I replied with apprehension.

"Oh, that's fantastic!" she beamed. "I've been trying to reach you for a very long time."

"I disappeared to the deep sea for a while, and I do travel everywhere either by swimming or by boat. It's only by chance that I'm near this cave. Have you been calling this phone the whole time?"

"...No," she replied unsteadily. "But anyway, please accept an invitation to my Sky Paradise above the clouds. You won't regret it!"

"Sky? Above the clouds?" I winced. I honestly had not been a fan of heights after my nightmarish experiences on the hill of the Island of the Fallen.

"Sky Paradise, yes," she reiterated. "I have a beautiful lake here, and you will love it!"

"How do I get there?" I questioned, wondering if perhaps hanging up the phone and swimming away was a better idea. I was persuaded by the thought of a beautiful lake, though.

"I'll send my giant albatross, it will be as simple as that," she chirped. "She will fly down in a few seconds. I am so looking forward to seeing you!"

I paddled back into the water and saw that outside the cave entrance, a white, majestic, giant albatross hovered above the ocean. She was waiting for me and was at least three times my size. There was no way I could have escaped her. Squawking loudly, she gestured for me to jump onto her back.

I had not realised just how scared of heights I was until her mighty wings carried me above the clouds. I closed my eyes and clung to her powerful neck and shoulders tightly, even when the albatross came to land on a grassy plateau. Once I knew we were on land, I clumsily rolled to the ground, collected myself and glanced around me.

The patch of grass that I was standing on was just one small part of what seemed to be a stunning 'roof' garden that carried on for miles. There were ornate waterfalls with elegant statues, exquisitely trimmed miniature trees and perfectly made pathways of pebbles that led winding routes through the lavish surroundings.

The garden seemed to be enjoyed by a plethora of different breeds of birds. Robins perched in the shrubbery, sparrows were snacking on bird feeders hanging from trees, and starlings swooped through the air in their graceful flocks. Colourful parrots and green conures chattered to each other in the tree branches. The sound was intoxicating - so many songs but so gently sung. It was indeed a paradise - if you liked birds, though.

There, clung to a wooden post where the path met the grass was a woman with short, spiked, platinum blonde hair. She wore a long, white, silk gown and boasted a pair of spotless, giant white wings. Her feet were not those of a human, though. They were akin to the intimidating claws of an eagle.

"Aqua Maddas!" she exclaimed with her chirpy, cheerful voice.

"Just call me Maddas," I replied with a sheepish smile, trying to stay calm around another 'creature', like myself, but so much more beautiful. "What's your name?"

"Flightsong. I am the Empress of the 'Sky Paradise'. Welcome to my home, and please make yourself comfortable here," she expressed warmly, her striking blue eyes were joyful and welcoming.

"Oh wow," I gasped, unable to hide how impressive I found her and her world. "I've met a couple of Queens, but I've never met an Empress before."

"Well, I rule an Empire of birds, not people," she clarified. "I have also been hiding from the war, and its consequences," she sighed sadly.

"It's a tough time to be a human," I commented.

"I have created this world somewhere perfect, free from conflict and cruelty. I hope you will enjoy your time here," Flightsong grinned proudly.

"It's an incredible place," I nodded, so overwhelmed that my voice sounded flatter than I had intended.

"You are not impressed?" she frowned.

"I assure you; I am very much impressed!" I replied with more enthusiasm, admiring the cornucopia of vibrant floral colours, and taking in the beautiful scents.

"You may relax here as long as you wish. The war has taken a heavy toll on the ocean, and on your health, I see," Flightsong offered, with a concerned tone.

"Oh, it's OK, I always look ill in comparison to humans," I reassured her. "But you're right - it's hard to swim anywhere without seeing so many shipwrecks and broken submarines full of human remains. It's horrifying."

"Indeed, it is."

"Anyway, you mentioned a lake? I would very much like to see it!" I grinned excitedly.

"Of course, follow me," Flightsong invited, flapping up into the air to lead me to one of the most exquisite bodies of water I had ever seen.

The water flowed down from a small mountain that climbed even higher into the clouds. At the base of that mountain, a peaceful waterfall with a pleasant rainbow fed freshwater into a crystalline lake. The water was so clear; I could see communities of carp and goldfish living a clean, idyllic existence. There were at least more than ten species of ducks and coots that made the lake their home. I chuckled with joy at seeing fuzzy ducklings and cute little moorhen chicks.

I lowered myself into the lake gently and instantly felt the healing powers of intense relaxation. Floating on my back, with the sound of birds chirping and little ducks quacking, I understood why the place was a paradise.

"The water here has curative properties. Bathe for as long as you want," Flightsong offered, grinning with glee at how much I sighed in pleasure whilst experiencing her well-created world.

"Why are you so kind to me?" I whispered.

"If you have to question kindness, then you need it the most," she replied.

"Wise," I acknowledged.

So, there I stayed in that wonderful Sky Paradise, enjoying the beautiful lake and an almost never-ending supply of healthy food in the form of nuts and seeds. I had made several aquatic bird friends and relished Flightsong's intelligent conversation.

Most of the time, Flightsong and I discussed our knowledge of seabird breeds, but that was stimulating enough for my fragile, recovering soul. There was a moment when I stared into Flightsong's caring, cerulean-coloured eyes that I thought I could feel love again, but it was still too soon after Yosef. My heart needed more time to heal, but at least the creepy tentacles on my head had receded.

After staying there for a little while, I noticed that mini storm clouds formed above the lake where I was swimming. Sometimes it would rain heavily in the patches of water where I sat and relaxed. It was enough to bring disorder to some coot nests. However, my mood was calm, and I was not consciously causing the storms.

Flightsong joined me beside the lake. I could tell from her expression that she was concerned about the violent weather that I had brought to her world.

"Um, Maddas," Flightsong chirped to me from the bank of the lake. "Would you mind not making rainstorms, please? I know that it is something that you sometimes do. But it is not really in keeping with this being, you know, a Paradise."

"Sorry, Flightsong, I do not mean to," I replied worriedly.

"Well, could you work out how to not make it stormy please?" she requested, politely but firmly.

"Normally, it takes a lot of energy for me to summon storms. I'm sorry, but I'm not sure why this is happening," I deliberated.

"Perhaps some residual trauma from the wars?" she suggested. "Maybe you could rest on the grass for a little bit. That always needs a bit of watering anyway."

"I can get out of the lake for a little bit, but honestly, I need to be in the water," I sighed sadly. "Perhaps I've outstayed my welcome?"

"No!" she replied suddenly, and then regained her composure. "Not at all. I'm sure we can work something out."

"If I'm causing you too much trouble, though..."

"As I said, I'm sure we can work something out," she smiled stiffly before flying away.

There was something about her voice which made me feel very odd. I tried to get back to relaxing and enjoying the pristine lake, but I could not shake an underlying worry.

It did not help the storm cloud situation either. The clouds just became thicker and brought down more rain. The coots started to avoid me, but at least the ducks were still my friends - for a little bit anyway. That was until sudden flashes of lightning leapt out from the clouds.

Flightsong came to join me beside the lake again when the thunder became unbearably loud.

"I am so sorry, Flightsong," I apologised sadly. "I don't know what's causing this."

"Do you want to talk about your pain?" she asked.

"I'm not sure I want to put my troubles on you. I carry many lifetimes of pain," I explained.

"It's no trouble for me at all. It's so lovely to have a friend who is so like me," she smiled.

"I think that we're quite different though. I'm all heavy and spiky. You're light and flappy."

I cursed myself at how awkward I was at coming up with compliments fitting such a beautiful being as Flightsong, but she laughed out loud. It felt good to make another soul feel happy again. The thunder and lightning began to recede as I started to feel calmer.

"I have studied your story. Birds have sung about you for thousands of generations," Flightsong informed.

"Surely not? I thought they were more interested in singing about food, territory and mating than an odd creature such as myself?" I questioned.

That is also true," Flightsong nodded. "Whatever they sing about, birdsong is the only music for me."

"No human music?"

"Music was taken from me, despite it being essential for my family. We were all musicians, but that was a long time ago. The war destroyed my entire family, except me, when I was a small child. Our enemies stole all of our riches and musical instruments," Flightsong explained.

"OK," I nodded, listening attentively. "It sounds like you've been through an awful time. I'm sorry."

"Well, just like you evolved and transformed yourself to escape from an Island that would have killed you if you didn't leave it, I also evolved. I remember that my enemies locked me in a cage like a little canary and tortured me. But I got through it by listening to the birdsong in the background. I wished so much that I could just grow wings and fly away. One day, after being beaten so hard that I almost died, I did just that. These gigantic wings grew out from my back, and my feet turned into sharp claws that pierced and stabbed my abusers before flying away."

"Wow," I gasped.

"I took to the sky and flew around the world, trying to find peace amidst the wars. I found this high plateau, secluded, and protected from everywhere else. It was a little world, just waiting for me to arrive. I moulded it to become my Sky Paradise, and now I live what seems to be an immortal life in a safe, beautiful place full of my favourite creatures. However, safety can become loneliness for supernatural beings like myself. I could not trust human beings ever again - not after what they did to me. So, when I heard about a 'Sea Creature' that became what they are due to a disturbing past, I knew I needed to meet you. I understand you, Maddas. I know that your Island of the Fallen story is all metaphor. We can heal our wounds, together, as best friends."

"My Island is not a metaphor," I replied quickly. "But I keep causing storms in your perfect world."

"I would like you to find a way to stop your storms. Perhaps you could talk to me more about your Island?" Flightsong probed.

"I don't think I'm ready to go into it yet," I decided. "I need to heal after losing Yosef first."

"The quicker you face it, the faster we can get rid of these unsightly storms," Flightsong pressed.

"I'm sorry, Flightsong," I sighed, clambering out of the lake. "I'm sorry for all that you have been through, but I don't think this is the place for me right now. I need to be back in my ocean and heal in my own time. I'm so grateful that you want to help me, though."

"No Maddas, you must stay. Please stay," Flightsong pleaded, before starting to sob.

"I'm just going to bring disorder to your world. Perhaps we could meet again - I can introduce you to the Listener. He's an excellent friend," I suggested.

"No! Stay!" Flightsong ordered sharply, kicking me back into the lake with a mighty claw before flying away.

I tried to climb out of the water again but realised that fearsome birds had surrounded the lake. Gigantic ostriches, emus and cassowaries marched around the body of water. When I turned back to the lake to search for another exit, I was joined by a bevy of aggressive swans, hissing at me to stay put.

"I should have predicted this would happen," I grumbled to myself. "I forgot that birds could be incredibly scary. No surprise they evolved from dinosaurs. I remember them being much worse monsters than myself."

To keep calm, I floated in the water for a little while, trying to work out what to do. I decided to have a go at reasoning with Flightsong. I stood up, with my webbed, clawed feet dug into the stony bottom of the lake.

"Look, Flightsong!" I shouted, hoping that she could hear. "I get it! I know what you feel! My hair became sticky tentacles, and I turned into something even more monstrous than I already am because I wanted to hold onto someone that I loved very much. I never wanted them to leave my life. Yosef was the first human person to make me feel accepted. I felt like I 'belonged' for the first time.

"But my loving feelings turned into something destructive, and I pushed him to have to defend himself from me at a time when he needed support, not possessive tentacle hair! I've worked through the pain, and now I'm just happy that I was able to have such a connection with a human, even if it was only for a short time relative to my lifespan. Maybe I will feel that way again, perhaps not. But I have learnt to let go. You've helped me to heal, but you need to let me go now!"

"Please don't leave me here, all alone," Flightsong sobbed, appearing suddenly on a tree branch nearby.

"Flightsong, by being in your Sky Paradise, you're *choosing* to be alone. I get it. I dived down to the deep ocean to isolate myself from a world I couldn't handle anymore. But eventually, one day, if you don't want to be alone, you must approach the world again. Gently, at first, and with slightly sharper claws, a thicker shell of spikes and hopefully more powerful foot-webbing."

Flightsong sighed angrily before flying away again. I didn't like to upset such an impressive being who had trusted me with her vulnerability, but her 'Paradise' was starting to feel more like the Island of the Fallen, just with a lot more beaks. I waited for a while, hoping that Flightsong would suddenly appear again and agree to take me back down to the ocean. When she did not, I decided that I needed to work out how to escape.

There was the violent option, with the likely result being the destruction of a beautiful place and the death of innocent creatures. Plus, without the albatross, I would have to jump from an excruciatingly frightening height, and I was not sure I would survive that. I wondered if I could grow wings, but it seemed to be something that I just could not do. There was a limitation to my evolutionary ability, after all.

I sank into the crystalline water of the lake and took some time to meditate on what I could do. There did not seem to be much choice apart from to look inward and explore my relationship with the water and the storms surrounding me. I could manipulate water, and I had done it many times before. I had become everything I was due to my affinity with water and the ocean. I listened to the water and felt that I had to trust my aquatic environment in what it was telling me to do.

In a sense, I had to forget what it was to be myself as a complete being. At first, I concentrated on my large, webbed hands. Meditating and breathing deeply, I watched as they started to dissolve. The cells that formed my skin, blood and bone separated themselves and detached from my body. They became single-celled organisms that floated in the water. As I drifted in the lake, my entire being slowly broke down to become microbes. I was entirely at one with the body of water as I disappeared into the liquid. In a sense, I felt myself becoming the lake itself.

"Goodbye, Flightsong," were the last words I spoke before I transformed myself.

I remember sensing Flightsong swooping around the lake in a panic, trying to figure out where I had gone. She called out to me, expecting a reply, but I could no longer talk. I had become something beyond myself.

Eventually, I started to elevate gradually by bioprecipitation. I floated up into the rain clouds hanging above the lake as the water evaporated. For a brief period, I almost felt the sensation of flying, but perhaps levitation was a more accurate description. I had no more fear of heights, just a feeling of peace as I was carried with the clouds whilst the wind pushed me away from the lake.

I was able to 'fly' away from Flightsong's world without her and her beaked army even realising that I had escaped. Although, it started to dawn on Flightsong when she gazed up at the storm cloud and saw it slowly drifting away from her. It did seem a little spiky, with edges that looked like arms, legs, and webbed claws.

The oddest feeling was when I slowly made my way back down to the ocean as part of every raindrop. Once each droplet met the sea, I steadily became reborn into my usual spiky, webbed, and gilled self.

However, something had changed in me. As I re-materialised, I felt relieved to be 'myself' again. I began to feel a sense of comfort in who I was and how I looked. Yes, I would probably not be able to blend in with ordinary human beings again, but I accepted myself, and that seemed to matter more. I do not think I can say that I learnt to truly 'love' myself, and I am not sure I will ever know how to do that. But I became able to appreciate every spike, every scale, every odd feature - even the tentacle 'hair' that appeared sometimes.

I rested on the little secluded cave beach where Flightsong's telephone was, letting my body's cells properly reform and re-attach themselves. After feeling more 'together', I was able to look at my reflection in the ocean, and not wish that I looked any different.

The telephone started to ring again, and for quite a while. However, I ignored it and slid back into the ocean to prepare myself for what I needed to do. It was time to face the repressed pain I felt from my past on the Island of the Fallen. That fear and anger still clung to me, much like my tentacle 'hair' did to Yosef. Those emotions would continue to bring storms that would follow me forever unless I did something about them."

"Did you ever face your Island?" Viktor asked Patient Seven, who was shocked that the Seahorse Boy was still listening to them.

"Well," Maddas began, but they were suddenly interrupted by the abrupt opening of the door behind them. Alice sprinted into the yard and leapt onto the tennis table. She made an impressive jump to the roof while wings sprouted out from her back.

"That's Alice! I told you!" Viktor cheered.

Whilst on the roof, Alice transformed herself into a dove, flapped her wings and took to the sky. In just a few seconds, she had disappeared from the ward.

"She will be back!" shouted Jeff menacingly from inside. "She's done this all before! She'll be back."

"This is why I won't escape," Maddas told Viktor. "I'm here for a reason, just like everyone else here."

Human Mermaids

"Psst! Maddas!" hissed Viktor, his head poking out from behind a wooden door to what Maddas thought was some sort of closet. "Join me in here! It's safe!"

Patient Seven tiptoed into the 'secret' room. It was the charmingly messy Art Room. Murals of trees had been painted on the walls, dotted with creations from patients past and present. Crucially, there was no one else there except for Viktor and Maddas. They could hide from some of the more dangerous patients who were on the prowl.

"The room is only accessible by the Nurses and particular patients. No having to worry about where Jeff is all the time in here," Viktor laughed. "Plus, I LOVE art."

Maddas gazed at an incredible drawing of a glamorous woman that Viktor had created.

"That is amazing!" Maddas exclaimed. "There is no way I can create anything that good!"

"Ah, it's nothing," Viktor blushed modestly.

"Is it a painting of someone in particular?" Maddas pried.

"...Yes," Viktor sighed. "Her name is Valerie - a sea nymph who stole my heart. But she disappeared from my life, leaving me heartbroken forever."

"Oh, I'm sorry," Maddas replied as softly as possible. "Do you want to talk about it?"

"Maybe later, not now," Viktor sniffed. "Who are you drawing?"

Maddas could tell that Viktor politely stifled a chuckle when viewing Patient Seven's rudimentary art skills.

"Her name is Selene," Maddas introduced. The rough drawing displayed a woman with long, wavy black hair and a beautiful, multi-coloured tail.

"Is she a mermaid?"

"Yes, the most beautiful mermaid I have ever encountered. I also do not know if I will ever see her again. Like most people I love, I tend to scare them away eventually."

"I get that," Viktor nodded empathetically, gesturing to his back, armed with many tiny but needle-sharp spines.

"I remember that it took me ages to find her," Maddas began.

"The process of rebuilding myself after escaping from Flightsong was one of the most exhausting feats I had ever accomplished. It felt as if I had become born again, both physically and mentally. Fortunately, it seemed like I had left behind all insecurities about myself and my body in Flightsong's crystal clear lake.

Plus, during re-composition, I had incorporated some algal cells into my being. Whilst taking a long nap on a sunny beach, the green algae in the non-scaly parts of my skin provided me with energy by photosynthesis, meaning I could go without food for extended periods. It was incredibly advantageous, mostly because I was too drained to hunt for food at that time.

During my long sleep, I had a remarkably vivid dream. In it, I saw a woman with long, black hair swimming around a kelp forest. She had a beautiful tail of vibrant red, pink, and cyan colours as if the most talented artist in existence had designed it. Towards the end of the dream, this mermaid swam close to me and screamed "you're the only one who can help me Aqua Maddas. Save me, and I can save you!"

I woke up suddenly as the tide began to encompass the beach. As usual, storm clouds were approaching me and bringing with them a more violent sea.

"Hmm, weird dream," I thought to myself. Believing it to be unimportant, I shrugged it off and prepared myself to get back to the ocean.

As I stood up, I realised that my body was still fragile. I could not walk properly without stumbling and falling over. There was also something very different about my mental state as well. I felt as though I was not entirely inhabiting my body all the time. Sometimes I felt as though a part of me was 'outside' of myself. That part of me seemed to be watching me as I tripped and fell headfirst on the beach.

I crawled my way up to the higher ground, feeling too vulnerable to be able to swim. From a small, grassy hill overlooking the beach, I watched the rough tide swallow the sand and wondered what to do next. What I needed was the Listener and his boat, but I had no idea where or when in the world he was. It had been such a long time since I had seen him. Feeling defeated, I collapsed on the grass and tried to calm myself by meditating.

There, I thought about the Listener and all the wonderful music he introduced to me. I so much wanted to see his hairy face and the often-disgruntled expressions he would make.

As I slipped into a slumber, the part of me that seemed to be 'outside' myself started to wander. It drifted through the sea, remembering all the different locations the Listener and I had travelled to, and all the interesting people we had met.

That incorporeal part of me swam up to the Listener in his boat, hopped aboard and tapped him on the shoulder whilst he deliberated about what record to play. He spun around with a confused frown, trying to work out what had happened or if someone had secretly boarded his boat to play tricks on him.

"I'm weak, Listener, and someone needs my help," I gasped, unsure if speaking would carry through to the detached part of myself.

Still sapped, I fell back into a deep slumber. I was not sure how long I was out for, but when I woke up next, it was to the sound of music playing from the sea. I sat up suddenly to see the Listener had arrived at the beach in his fantastic, magical music boat.

"I reached you! Somehow I reached you!?" I cried as I flopped down the side of the grassy hill to get to the boat. I was surprised not just by what had happened, but also by the fact that I was still able to swim despite my crippling exhaustion. The Listener helped me back into the boat and scratched his hairy head as I collapsed in a heap on the deck.

He was deep in thought for a couple of seconds before then shrugging and going back to deciding which melody was the one to play next. As if the day could not get any stranger, the record he chose had a picture of a mermaid on it not too dissimilar from the one in my dream.

"I saw her! I saw that mermaid in a dream! She's in trouble. What is going on? What is happening to me?" I exclaimed, finding it a challenge to process everything that had occurred.

The Listener shrugged again and decided to play the record. We were quickly transported away from the stormy beach to a much calmer sea, and it meant that I could study the picture of the mermaid with a bit more concentration.

"Is she underwater here? I need to help her," I demanded, readying myself to dive into the ocean.

The Listener placed his hand on my arm, gesturing for me to calm myself. Despite his silence, his knowing gaze communicated to me that I still needed to rest. He pointed towards the sky, in which thick clouds were continuing to follow us, and then tapped me on the forehead. He was trying to say to me that I needed to mend my mental state. At least, that was what I thought.

"I will face my troubles when I'm ready. Right now, I need to help someone. I think I need to find them before I even try to face my past," I argued. The storm clouds seemed to stay put but still threatened to bring a torrent of rain at any moment.

The Listener shook his head, looking frustrated at being misunderstood. He tapped me on the forehead again, and then placed the palm of his hand there. Through a series of hand gestures, he communicated to me that I still needed to rest but that I could use my new ability to dissociate to search for the mermaid without having to expend my physical energy.

"You know, sometimes I bet you wish you could talk," I chuckled. "I'm not sure if I have asked you before, but why can't you talk?"

The Listener frowned angrily for a couple of seconds before doing his usual shrug.

"OK mermaid, I will find you," I told myself as I lay back on the deck while holding the record cover picture of the mermaid. My mind tapped into the music that the Listener was playing. I heard soothing yet sad female vocals from an aquatic being who was singing for our help.

I let my mind wander and detach from my body again, letting it drift down into the sea. My incorporeal self swooped through a kelp forest that was eerily like the one in my dream. I must have searched the kelp for an hour, as well as dived down to the darker depths. However, I could not find the mermaid, so I retrieved my incorporeal self back to my body.

"Can't find her down below," I reported to the Listener, who stroked his hairy cheeks and beard whilst deep in thought.

I meditated on the word 'mermaid' for a little while and wondered where my thoughts would take me. My mind brought me visions of a group of women diving into the ocean, hunting for oysters and particular types of seaweed. On collecting what they wanted, they would swim up to store their catchings on a small boat. I woke up suddenly after bringing my incorporeal self back to me.

"I'm not sure I saw mermaids, but I saw some people who might know about them," I suggested to the Listener. He interrupted me to point towards the sky. The storm clouds had reached our boat, bringing with them heavy rainfall and a turbulent sea.

"The women I saw - I think they were Japanese?" I pondered. "Let's go and find them!"

The Listener put his hand on my head again, suggesting I use the power of my mind once more.

"It's a fun new skill, but I still want to meet people in person. I want to feel like I *exist*," I explained.

The Listener sighed wearily before looking in his box of records for Japanese music. To the sound of upbeat Japanese melodies, we travelled to the sea that framed the Shima Peninsula of Japan. Although the Listener was still keen that I rested, it was important to me to regain my swimming and diving strength. I jumped into the ocean to explore and to meet the creatures that lived in and around the pink, purple and orange corals underwater.

There, I met vibrant yellow frogfish and admired their somewhat disgruntled-looking expressions. Bright orange seahorses and psychedelic nudibranchs added even more intensity to the beautiful pigmentation of my surroundings. Friendly, stripy bullhead sharks swam up to meet me and examined my odd self.

As I had hoped, I was not the only individual diving around the reefs. A couple of women, dressed in all-white wetsuits, joined me under the water. They wore fins on their feet as well as round masks to protect their eyes and faces. They were collecting particular types of seaweed, oysters, and other shellfish from the reef before swimming up towards what seemed to be a small boat, as I had seen in my earlier visions.

I met them at the surface in the hope of making a connection, although they were very busy. They whistled to each other before quickly diving back into the water again, resurfacing and depositing their collections into the small white boat.

"Um, hello there," I greeted them, attempting to speak Japanese. One of the women saw me and looked terrified. In hindsight, perhaps I should have transformed myself into a more human-like appearance as I had done before. However, that would have been tiring after re-forming my body.

"Tomokazuki!" one of the women cried, before climbing up into their boat. Other women shouted the same as they surfaced.

"Wait, I'm Aqua Maddas! I bring you no harm! I just want to talk please," I tried.

"What are you?" one woman asked.

"I'm a sea creature, and I'm very much harmless. I have a boat as well with my friend the Listener," I explained, pointing to my fluffy friend as he drifted towards us, still playing Japanese music. I jumped into the Listener's boat and let one of the women tie their vessel to ours.

"We are the Ama. Ama means 'women of the sea' in Japanese. Our diving culture is thousands of years old, and we have seen many strange things in the ocean. Although, you might be one of the weirdest," chuckled an elderly woman who seemed to oversee the group. "Would you like a sea snail, Aqua Maddas?"

"Absolutely! Thank you!" I exclaimed, crunching on a deliciously fresh mollusc. "Please, just call me Maddas."

"My name is Yoshiko. What do you want to talk to us about?" the elderly woman asked. "Better make it quick - I can see storm clouds approaching."

"Oh, not again!" I grumbled. "Are you mermaids by any chance?"

"People have often called us that," Yoshiko laughed. "We are completely human women though, but with thick skin and a strong sense of community. We have adapted so that we can dive in these cold waters."

I picked up the record cover that displayed the picture of the mermaid.

"Have you seen any mermaids before? Like this one?" I questioned.

"Perhaps after drinking too much sake," Yoshiko joked. "No, I have not seen anything like her before." The other women of the group also looked at the picture and shook their heads.

"You might want to ask the Haenyeo," one of the women suggested. "They dive around the Island of Jeju, near South Korea."

"Thank you," I smiled, bowing to them out of respect. "I hope you continue with your traditions of diving."

"One thing, before you go," Yoshiko interrupted. "When you do find this mermaid, will you want to give her a gift?"

"You know what, maybe?" I pondered.

"We are world-famous for our ability to pearl dive," she began. "You look like a very effective diver too. If you help us out with today's hunt before the storm clouds ruin our day, we will let you have one of our oyster pearls."

"That sounds like a lot of fun and a good deal for everyone involved," I smiled in agreement. The Listener rolled his eyes wearily and pointed to the grey clouds that had appeared above us.

I dove back into the water, accompanying our new friends on their watery hunt. Whilst I kept close to these impressive humans and their brilliant white attire, I learnt that they were particularly interested in hunting for wriggly sea cucumbers and large, spiky, turban-shell sea snails. They were armed with sharp knives and used them to pull sea creatures out from rocks or thick clumps of seaweed. It was incredibly gratifying to use my own sharp claws in a way that could benefit humanity instead of scaring it.

"Do you humans have gills?" I asked the women as I threw most of my catch into their boat. On occasion, I would snack on some spare sea cucumbers to regain my energy.

"Haha, we wish," one of the divers chuckled before disappearing back into the water.

They would sometimes be swimming underwater for more than a minute, and I was astounded to realise that these humans had not evolved gills.

"If you humans keep diving, you'll get your gills one day for sure," I winked at Yoshiko who humoured me with a wry smile.

After about two hours of diving and hunting, I was surprisingly exhausted but happy to have had such a great time with these human mermaids. The storm clouds above thickened and rumbled ominously whilst we sat in our tied, anchored boats.

"I think it's time to call it a day," Yoshiko suggested. "Is that storm something to do with you, Maddas?"

"...Perhaps a little," I admitted as the Listener nodded determinedly. "I didn't see any oysters today though. Does that mean no pearls for the mermaid I'm supposed to find?"

"Haha, you think we would reveal to you the locations of the pearl-bearing oysters?" Yoshiko laughed. "For a sea monster, you are quite funny."

"Well, then I take back my sea cucumbers!" I grumbled with a jokey frown.

"Calm down, Maddas," Yoshiko sighed. "You may have this one."

Yoshiko outstretched her arm and placed a beautiful pearl into the palm of my webbed hand.

"Consider this as an offering to the sea," Yoshiko uttered. "May the ocean provide good hunting for many more generations."

"I will do my best to make that happen," I expressed whilst I inspected the precious stone.

"Thank you so much for this. Wow, this pearl is magnificent!"

"All we ask in return is for you to help keep our culture alive," Yoshiko requested. "And please stop that storm from coming our way."

"No problem. We will leave immediately and visit the Haenyeo, that will help," I decided quickly.

"Enjoy meeting the Haenyeo! Say 'hello' from me!" Yoshiko cried out.

"I hope we will. Let's get some Jeju music playing!" I commanded the Listener. "Thank you and goodbye!"

I searched the boat for a safe place to keep the pearl. The Listener scratched his fluffy black mane and gestured to a small hidden compartment within the record player. I hid the pearl and waved goodbye to Yoshiko, and the rest of the Ama divers whilst the Listener huffed to himself before playing the song 'Ieodo Sana'.

The enrapturing tune made us disappear almost immediately from Japanese waters and into the Korea Strait sea. There we drifted near to the coast of Jeju island, and I began searching for another group of extraordinary sea women.

Underwater, shoals of striped fish and jellyfish swam about an abundance of more pink and purple corals. There was no sign of divers yet. However, when I surfaced, I noticed that a small portion of rice and eggs was sailing towards my face. I gobbled up the welcome surprise without much hesitation.

Our boat met a rocky shore, where we spotted a group of women wearing black diving suits, sitting inside a round, rocky structure. We heard them singing and chatting together. Some of them were placing small offerings of food into the sea. Although I wanted to take more food, I decided not to and instead focused on approaching the women with care and caution. I noticed that some of the women had sharp, metallic spears or piercing hunting knives. The Listener patted my shoulder in a way that warned me to be careful.

"Um, hello," I greeted the group awkwardly. "Thank you for the eggs!"

Expecting shock, disbelief and perhaps learning of another sea deity, I was amazed that the women seemed completely unphased by me. They carried on singing together. Some women were busy opening shellfish to get at their soft, edible flesh.

"Are you the Haenyeo?" I asked them.

One of the women gestured for me to sit next to them. I sat down carefully beside them on a rock and graciously accepted some of their fresh shellfish.

"I am Chun-ja, but you should address me as 'Sanggon'. I am a leader of the Haenyeo. The goddesses and gods of the sea visit us in many ways. What is your message?" the woman asked. Like the other women, she was wearing a thick, black wetsuit with a round diving mask positioned on her forehead for the time being. Her face was freckled and displayed many stories in the form of beautiful laughter lines.

"I'm Aqua Maddas, and I have no message, I don't think," I mumbled. "I'm looking for a mermaid. She has black hair and a multicoloured tail - I can show you a picture of her if you need?"

"We are the only mermaids you'll find here," Chun-ja chuckled. The other women laughed with her. "I've seen many things - sea dragons, the spirits of past Haenyeo and the Goddess Yeongdeung, but I have not met women with tails. At least from what I remember."

Some of the women stood up to leave the rocks. They fastened their masks over their faces and carried with them orange floats with large nets tied to them, ready for their underwater hunt.

"Are you going to dive with them?" I asked Chun-ja.

"I am in my nineties," she replied wistfully. "I swim mainly in the shallows, and my diving days are in the past. My role now is to provide advice and maintain order."

She let out a thoughtful sigh.

"But I do miss it," she murmured. "Despite the heavy toll diving has taken on my body. Despite the cold and the rough seas, I do miss the hunt."

"If you'd like to dive again, I can escort you?" I suggested. "I'd make sure that you get back safely."

"I shouldn't…" she thought. "Oh, but I would very much like that."

"Take my hand," I offered. Chun-ja held my webbed hand with a strong clench as we stepped carefully over the rocks to get to the sea. I waved and gave a thumbs-up to the Listener who patiently waited in the boat, with a slightly disgruntled expression as usual.

I let Chun-Ja lead the way into the sea as she gestured towards areas known to have vibrant reefs full of sea life. Her pupils dilated with the thrill of being able to see the underwater paradise again. She must have been delighted to have someone doing most of the swimming for her as well. The other Haenyeo divers swam near to us as they gathered shellfish and more sea cucumbers from the ocean floor. We heard their whistle calls as they surfaced.

Bottlenose dolphins joined us as we swooped around the crimson reefs. They seemed to recognise Chun-Ja as if she were an old friend of theirs. We sighted vivid orange, blue and yellow sea slugs crawling around the underwater vegetation. Chun-Ja tapped my arm to signal caution as we swam near to a tiny but deadly blue-ringed octopus.

On surfacing, I noticed that storm clouds had found us once more. The Listener pointed towards the sky to make it known that I should leave the area to protect the Haenyeo. For a second, I became aware that Chun-Ja was no longer holding my claw. I panicked and dived back into the water to search for her.

I re-traced our journey and thought about where she could have gone. Eventually, I found her swimming underwater and determinedly following what I thought was a long fish, possibly a large eel. I swam up beside her and took her hand. She pointed towards the creature, which was not an eel - it was a turquoise dragon! It winded its way around the reefs and seemed to disappear into the distance. I grabbed Chun-Ja's hand and pulled her to the surface.

"I saw the Sea Dragon," Chun-Ja gasped. "I must follow it to what awaits me."

"I promised you that I would get you back safely," I cried. "Let's get you onto the Listener's boat."

The Listener came to collect us. I offered to help Chun-Ja into the boat, but she adamantly climbed into the vessel without much aid.

"For some reason, a storm is following me," I admitted to Chun-Ja. "I need to get you safely back to shore and then leave before the storm finds me."

"OK," she sighed, frowning angrily at me for a while. Eventually, she eased.

"You're right. I must be the Sanggon and lead the Haenyeo for as long as I can. One day I will follow the Sea Dragon and see where it leads me. But for now, thank you for the dive, Aqua Maddas."

"I'm glad I helped you enjoy the sea once more," I smiled, embracing Chun-Ja.

"You know who could help you find your Mermaid? The Bajau people, or the Sea Nomads. They live around Indonesia, Malaysia and the Philippines," Chun-Ja suggested once she arrived back on land. "Perhaps they will know?"

The Listener tutted to himself as I gave him an excited smile.

"I know it's a long shot, but they might have the answer. It doesn't hurt to try, and I like visiting aquatic humans," I persuaded him. "Let's go to Indonesia!"

Selene

"Did the Bajau people help you find her?" Viktor asked Maddas. They were still spending peaceful, quality time in the Art Room, with Patient Seven continuing to draw pictures of the Mermaid close to their heart.

"The Listener and I had a fantastic time with the Bajau people, although they prefer to be called the 'Sama'," Maddas informed.

"Makeshift spear in hand, I hunted the reefs of the Banda Sea alongside the 'Sea Nomads'. They were such fascinating people in that they could walk on the seafloor very swiftly. I had not seen many human beings with that ability.

They let me use one of their metallic spear guns and encouraged me to do away with my usual rudimentary spears. The only other equipment they had were wooden goggles to protect their eyes, although sometimes they would not even need those. Like the Ama and the Haenyeo, the Sama Sea Nomads could make their dives sometimes last more than three minutes.

After catching a healthy amount of fish and octopuses, I stayed with the Sama in their wooden stilt houses built above the sea. In between mouthfuls of succulent fresh fish, the Listener and I learnt about their culture. Although they were incredibly welcoming and had many exciting stories to tell me, they had no idea about any mermaid. I was the closest thing they had seen to a mermaid, although they often referred to me as a 'Jinn' or a sea spirit.

They were happy for me to stay with them for as long as possible, but as storm clouds continuously followed me, I felt I needed to leave before bringing disruption to the community. I promised them that once I had found the Mermaid and solved my storm problem, I would return to hunt with them again. They did warn me that their sea nomad culture was slowly disappearing, so I made sure to assure them that I would tempt them back to the sea if need be.

The Listener and I disappeared to a part of the Pacific Ocean far away from any land and waited for the storm clouds to find us. The Listener stood with his arms folded, adamant that I face my storm and listen to what it was trying to communicate to me.

I lay on the wooden deck of the Listener's boat and gazed up at the gloomy, dark grey clouds that eventually caught up to us. As frosty rainwater fell whilst the clouds rumbled violently, I began to receive visions of the Island of the Fallen. I remembered the Grip of the forest, where vines lashed at me, attempting to bind my arms and legs to trap me. I saw the cave full of skeletons, and I heard the nightmarish screams amidst the hypnotic singing that travelled through the air of the Island.

"I can't do it!" I cried as I sat up suddenly, holding my head in my webbed hands. "I can't face it yet! I am not strong enough! I can't do this alone!"

The Listener patted my shoulder, his eyes looking more sympathetic.

"I know the Island of the Fallen is calling me back," I sobbed, my body shaking with fear. "It wants me to explore the caves under the hill. I'm not ready."

As the rain thudded around me and the sea became more violent, the Listener slid about the boat attempting to get us away from the storm. I lay down on the deck again, trying to connect to the clouds and the wind.

Searching my memories, I recalled when the storm pushed me away from my Island out to sea. I remembered my time on the rock and the gradual process of becoming 'Aqua Maddas'. My mind drifted to the hill of the Island, and the stern, stony Golem that inhabited it. That creature was calling me back.

"*Aqua Maddas, your training is complete. It is time to accept your fate. You must find your purpose before it's too late,*" the Golem chanted. "*Face your fears and come back to the cave, you have here the belonging you crave.*"

"I belong here in the sea!" I yelled.

The chants of the Golem faded as I began to hear a much more beautiful sound. I listened to the singing resonate to me from the sea, and I recognised that the voice belonged to the mermaid from my visions. She was calling to me.

"I need help Aqua Maddas," she sang. "Help me, and I will help you face your Island."

"Can you hear her singing?" I asked the Listener, who nodded. "We need to find her!"

Our boat vanished from the stormy sea and reappeared near to the coast of an island. It was not the Island of the Fallen, but it was presumably the location of the troubled mermaid.

The island itself looked intriguing. Broken slabs of rock littered a sandy beach overlooked by a small cliff. Carved into the side of the cliff edge was a cracked stone archway that framed a hidden enclave. Beside the archway, a fractured staircase led up from the beach to the clifftop, where the ruins of an old temple resided. It was as if we had arrived at an abandoned, ancient civilisation.

I dived into the sea to find that the oceans hid the remains of a settlement. Algae and black, spiky anemones covered deformed statues, incomplete walls, and timeworn bridges. An almost intact stone 'house' had become the home to a rather large octopus who seemed displeased about being disturbed. As I perched on the algae-coated roof of the 'house', cuttlefish scuttled away from me towards better hiding places. I peered around at my surroundings, hoping to catch sight of the mermaid.

Instead of seeing the mermaid, I drifted into a meditative state of mind. My eyes caught shadowy figures moving around the submerged ruins. Shoals of fish journeyed through the sea but seemed to wind around the shadows. I had stumbled upon an underwater city of souls that clung to a world lost to the tides.

In the corner of my eye, and well hidden amongst the shadows, I caught sight of a rainbow coloured tail. It belonged to the mermaid from my dreams! After shaking myself out of meditation, I tried to follow the mermaid, but she disappeared all too quickly. I traced her movements and realised that she had climbed out of the water and onto the beach. Her tail had rapidly transformed into human legs once she was on dry land. She ran towards the steps leading up to the cliff and scaled them at an impressive speed.

"Hello!" I called, though she seemed to ignore me. She appeared to be in a rush to get back to somewhere.

I sat on the rocky beach munching on an anemone. The Listener waved to me, but I gave him a shrug. The situation was incredibly confusing, so I decided to explore the beach to collect more information.

The archway beckoned to me, so I examined it. The enclave behind it was empty apart from a pile of dried seaweed, pebbles, and some seashells. My only company was a shy lizard that scuttled to a hiding place in one of the cracks of the grey-white walls. I looked up to see that there was some faded artwork, just above my line of sight.

The painting depicted the mermaid with her distinctive multicoloured tail, sitting next to a king with a gold crown and a long, black gown. The king's hands clasped around the neck of the mermaid. In between the king and the mermaid was a much smaller figure. That figure had turquoise skin, webbed feet, and spiky shoulders.

"I think that's me," I muttered to myself.

I waited on the beach until nightfall, sheltered underneath the archway. Letting myself relax a little, I enjoyed gazing up at the full moon and twinkling stars that were also reflected by the ocean tides. I became subdued by the sounds of the sea as well of the songs of crickets in the dry grass next to the archway and soon fell asleep. The next thing I knew was that I was woken up suddenly by a kiss on the forehead from a woman with long, black wavy hair and hazelnut-coloured eyes.

"You finally found me," she chuckled happily. Her face was round, with her pale skin illuminated by the light of the moon. She appeared to be wearing a rainbow-coloured dress, much like the colours of the mermaid's tail.

"Are you the mermaid I saw in my dream?" I asked.

"It wasn't a dream," she informed me. "We connected by the power of our minds. Aqua Maddas, you're finally beginning to understand who you are and find your true purpose."

"What's your name?"

"Selene," she replied. Her elegant name matched her astonishing beauty.

"You said you needed my help, Selene?" I replied.

"Yes, and I think I can help you too," she smiled.

"Why did you run away from me?" I quizzed. "Also, where are we? Are we in the ruins of a ghost city?"

"I was not running away from you. I had to get back to the city before anyone suspected anything," she explained.

"Oh, OK. I thought I might have scared you with my monstrous self."

"Monstrous?" she frowned and then laughed. "I've never perceived you as a monster. What are you though?"

"I'm just a sea...creature," I shrugged awkwardly. Selene's beauty and presence affected my poise and made it a challenge to find my words.

"I know that you're from the Island of the Fallen," she spoke. "I know that it's calling for you."

"Yes, that's true," I gasped. "Do you know that Island? How do you know all this?"

"Mermaids are as ancient as you are. Songs about the sea and all of its inhabitants are passed from mermaid to mermaid throughout history," she explained. "Sometimes that Island calls to us too. There is a prophecy tied to it, but I know that you are not ready for it, just as I am not yet ready to face my foe."

"I saw the artwork. Are you in trouble with some sort of king? Is that why you want my help?"

"There are many misconceptions about mermaids. Mermaids were blamed for the sea taking half of the Island, but it was not us. The people of this city were miners, and their activities polluted the ocean. The sea fights a continual battle with humanity and takes from the humans when it needs to. Mermaids do what they can to restore the balance, by planting corals and clearing up waste. However, the trapped souls of this city would rather blame the mermaids for the wrath of the sea. The King of this island hates me and wants to get rid of me. He knows that I am a mermaid, although I try to hide it when I'm on land," Selene explained.

"Hmm," I replied, taking in what she was saying. I had a feeling that she was withholding some information.

"Humans think of mermaids as 'takers' or 'monsters. It's far from the truth," she elaborated. Her voice was akin to soothing music.

"Well, you're the first mermaid I've met, so I don't hold such preconceptions," I assured her. "Also, I know how it feels to be misjudged. There are millions of songs describing me as a 'Sea Devil' or an evil, scary creature when all I've tried to do is make friends with humans."

"There are millions of mermaid songs about humans being more monstrous than you, Maddas," she informed me.

"I'll ask the Listener to play some," I grinned. "Anyway, what can I do to help you?"

"As I mentioned, the King here hates mermaids. He is planning to catch me after one of my swims and kill me. He often patrols the beach and the cliff in the early morning, waiting for me. Can you do something to scare him away?" she requested, placing her delicate hands on my spiky shoulders.

"I can certainly try, Selene," I replied nervously.

"Help me beat him, and I will help you face your Island," she added.

Selene gave me another kiss on my forehead with her velvety lips before vanishing from sight, into the ocean.

So, I waited at the shore all night, gorging on anemones and shellfish as the tide rose. I climbed the unsteady steps and took a look at the temple ruins at the top of the cliff, still watching out for the King but also gazing to the sea in the hope that I would see Selene again.

I could only stay on land for so long. Once the morning sun started to illuminate the beach, I waded back into the seawater. As I splashed about in the shallows with my webbed claws, I chuckled at small fish following my feet. The shoals were attracted to the tiny shrimp kicked up by my strides. It gave me an idea. I examined my reflection and wondered if perhaps I could act as 'bait' for the King by changing my appearance in some way. Maybe I could become more 'mermaid-like'?

My usually short and messy, green-coloured hair grew longer and boasted some 'highlights' in the form of purple and cyan tentacles. My eyelids sprouted enhanced eyelashes, my lips became more voluminous, and my chest moulded itself into a full cleavage. I even wrapped seaweed around myself to accentuate my figure.

I took a moment to admire my new physique, but soon caught sight of a threatening pair of black eyes. At the top of the cliff beside the ruined temple, there he stood, wearing his gold crown and black cloak. He seemed to be carrying a metal staff. Moments later, I realised that the staff was a spear that he had launched towards me.

I swerved out of the way as it shot through the water, but then I spun around and grabbed hold of the spear. Before striding towards land, I glanced at myself in the water. I was a mixture of sea-monster and frightening 'sea-witch', and I felt satisfied with my appearance. The power I had gained from enhancing my feminine attributes made me feel stronger and more confident in myself.

With a surge of energy, I ran to the beach and sprinted towards the King as fast as my long-webbed feet would allow. Still wielding the spear, I clashed with the King. He attacked me with two rapidly drawn rapier swords and certainly impressed me with his ability to dual wield. I defended myself with the spear and pushed him back with a powerful kick from my right foot. The King stepped back but then lunged at me with his swords as I veered to the side.

"What ARE you?" yelled the King - his fearsome black eyes conveyed that he wished to end me. "Are you a monster? Are you a man? Are you a woman?"

He swung his swords at me again, and I managed to kick one blade from out of his hand.

"I don't quite know!" I shouted back. "Why do you want to kill the mermaid?!"

I leapt at the King and caught him in a headlock. On restraining him, I managed to pry the other sword from his hand. I pushed him to the ground and roared at him, baring my sharp teeth.

"Why do you care? She's a troublemaker and not important like a King!"

"Honestly, I wish you humans would stop trying to hurt and kill everything," I grumbled. "Just sit down, relax, listen to a bit of music, float on the water and calm your thoughts. Killing someone else is not always the answer!"

"I will kill you, whatever you are! Sea Demon? Sea Witch?" he yelled.

"I believe you tried and failed. Now, let's sit here and talk about exactly why you want to kill the mermaid," I proposed.

We sat on the edge of the cliff watching the sunrise and enjoyed seeing the warm light enliven the pristine water of the ocean below. Whilst I transformed back into my everyday appearance, he told me about his riches, his dynasty, his castle at the centre of the island and his royal family. He regaled me with his hunting adventures and how he had been able to have everything and anything he wanted and lived in a palace full of gold.

"The mermaid is my one weakness. She took half of my city from me and submerged it in the ocean. If I do not kill her first, she will take me and the rest of the city with her," he growled.

I took a moment to glance behind us at the rest of the island. In the light, all I could see were more ruins. There had been a civilisation once, but time and the ocean had eroded this ancient city. The vague outlines of houses could be mistaken for piles of rocks.

"Am I missing something here? Is there a city now, or is it in a different time dimension?" I frowned.

"My city is one of the best in the world," he stated confidently. I smiled awkwardly to humour him.

"Are you sure that killing the mermaid is the best course of action?" I reasoned.

"Of course!" he yelled.

I decided to be like the Listener and let the silence do the talking whilst the King wrestled with his thoughts.

"OK, maybe not," he sighed. "Don't tell anyone I said this, but I both hate and admire her. The mermaid is everything that I am not, and she is better than I could ever be. She knew that an earthquake would come and cause the sea to take half of my city. She knows that there is nothing left here. I cling to these ruins and the shadows of the people that think of me as a King. The mermaid is so free, so caring and so determined to make things better."

"Ah, so perhaps you're in love with her?"

"I'm not sure. She can never truly be a part of my Kingdom, though. Her true home is in the sea. To accept her would mean I give up everything here."

"I'm perplexed," I winced. "So, is that why you want her gone?"

Our conversation was interrupted by the rumble of clouds above.

"Oh, and I'm very sorry, but it's going to rain now. I can't seem to do anything to stop that," I warned.

As the rain began to fall, I started to notice how feminine the King's eyes were.

"I would rather let the mermaid go than be reminded of what I have lost here. I don't want to let go of everything I have achieved and all that I am."

He released his black hair, which I had only just noticed was tied in a tight ponytail. Beneath his gown, a rainbow tail replaced his feet. He tried to grab one of his swords back, although I swiped it from his, now her, exquisitely delicate hand with pink-painted nails.

"Look, you can be anything you want to be," I explained, beginning to understand the situation. "What's the point in royalty and prestige? When I travelled along the bottom of the ocean, I saw many shipwrecks. Some of these wrecks contained chests full of coins, bars of gold and jewellery full of diamonds. Treasure did not stop those ships from sinking and did not prevent humans from dying. The best thing you can do is live your life and enjoy it as much as you can and not get tied by status and possessions."

"But will people accept me? How can anyone accept me if I cannot accept myself?"

"Accepting yourself is the first and most important thing, although it is not easy. However, it is more important than having others accept you, in my opinion," I shared, taking hold of the King's delicate hand. "I promise you that I accept you for whoever you are and whoever you want to be."

"Thank you," the King smiled, removing the crown from his head, and revealing herself to be the beautiful mermaid that had been kept hidden for so long. The King had transformed into Selene, their true self, and sighed with relief.

As the rain beat down upon the island, shadows emerged from the city ruins and travelled with the flowing rainwater, down into the sea. We watched from the cliff as the shadows from land joined those in the submerged city. The once trapped souls rose to the sea surface and vanished into the crashing waves, letting go of their past lives.

I waved to the Listener who had been waiting patiently in his boat anchored to the bay. Selene and I jumped into the sea as the tides rose and joined the Listener. We both climbed aboard the cabin cruiser and helped my furry friend choose a record that would help us leave the storm-beaten island.

"This is my friend, the Listener," I introduced to Selene. "I hope you like every single genre of music?"

"Wow, you always tell the most amazing stories," Viktor gasped. "That's your talent. More so than your art if I'm honest."

"I think I just need some practice," Maddas laughed, looking at the disordered picture of Selene.

There was a sudden knock on the Art Room door.

"Maddas, you have a visitor," a Nurse called.

Maddas exited the Art Room cautiously and made their way to the entrance of the ward, followed by a curious Viktor. Standing near the door to the outside world was a woman with long black hair, pale skin, and bright red lips.

"Selene!" Maddas cried. "See, Viktor, this is the mermaid I was telling you about!"

Patient Seven hugged the slightly distressed woman.

"Hey, you," she smiled awkwardly. "Um, I brought you some biscuits."

Part 3: The Reason

How Monstrous

Patient Seven lay curled up on their side on a small bench in the corridor beside their room. They gripped their knees and muttered to themselves. Viktor joined them and stroked their spiky shoulder soothingly but with care, thankful that their claws were tough enough not to get cut by Maddas's spikes.

"What's wrong?" Viktor asked. "You seemed so happy to see Selene."

"Yes, but it's hard seeing her so upset and in pain," Maddas sobbed. "She doesn't like seeing me in here, and I've been such an awful person towards her. She deserves better than to be with a monster like me."

"Well, whatever has happened, she cares about you a lot, and it seems as though she wants to help you get out of here," Viktor added.

"I'm not meant to be released yet," Patient Seven sighed.

"What happened between you and her? Is it part of the reason why you are in here?" Viktor asked.

"I can't quite remember," Maddas frowned. "Well, I can't remember *everything.*"

"I remember that the best thing about being with the mermaid, Selene, was that we could both share our love of the ocean. I showed her my favourite locations and introduced her to the animals I had bonded with on previous adventures. We were partly searching for the Island of the Fallen, but our journey became more about exploring the world's seas. In fact, for a while, our time was not marred by the arrival of storms. We had perfect weather and an idyllic existence, even if only for a short time.

We swam with dolphins in the Atlantic, with turtles and hammerhead sharks in the Red Sea, and with cute, mischievous seals in the North Sea. Selene revealed to me some locations that she thought would interest me. For instance, she made me aware of an entire 'reef' of toilet bowls at Ras Mohammed in the Red Sea.

We laughed at each other as we posed, looking 'human-like' whilst sitting on toilets that had littered the sea from a past shipwreck. However, that moment sparked uneasy emotions within me about the relationship between humanity and our ocean home. I hoped that those emotions would dissipate, but that was not the case at all.

I took Selene to the Great Barrier Reef, hoping to impress her with the cornucopia of colour and life. However, what I saw began to turn my mood sour. Years ago, the reef was utterly stunning and brimming with an almost unlimited diversity of wildlife and vibrancy. However, at the time we had arrived, the corals had become bleached white. It was as if we had emerged at a graveyard full of coral skeletons devoid of life.

"What happened to this place?" I grumbled to Selene and the Listener as we took a break aboard the boat. We were weary from searching for any signs of life on the reef.

"Coral bleaching," Selene answered, with the Listener nodding in agreement. "The world is getting warmer. I believe this is due to humankind."

Throughout history, I had always tried to see the best in humans. I wanted to connect with them so much that I looked past the weapons, the destruction, and the occasional cruelty. There had undoubtedly been times that I felt angry with them. I had been furious about oil spills, the dumping of toxic pollutants into rivers and how populations of fish could be entirely decimated by humans fishing for more than is necessary. However, the ocean always found a way to adapt and bounce back. The seas would change and evolve, just like myself.

However, on my adventures with Selene, the frequency at which we encountered humanity's wrecking of the sea meant that I could no longer ignore what I was seeing. When Selene wanted to relax on beaches, we often came across enormous piles of plastic rubbish scattered around the sands and pebbles. Hermit crabs would find homes in plastic cups and bottle-caps. Sometimes we watched from afar as humans cut open deceased beached whales who had stomachs full of plastic waste.

On our adventures in the Pacific Ocean, Selene, the Listener, and I came across gigantic floating patches of plastic rubbish. Bottles, bags, and tubing had become trapped in discarded nets, as well as the carcasses of imprisoned dolphins, turtles, and sharks. I became overwhelmed with grief for the animals that had succumbed to a foe that I had no idea how to defeat.

"Everywhere I go, I see the ocean suffering," I sobbed to Selene after avoiding being caught in netting myself. "I feel personally attacked. Every animal that dies from all this pollution feels like a punch to the face."

As I lay on the deck of the boat, removing pieces of plastic and stray netting from my claws, storm clouds found us and threatened to match my turbulent mood.

"Let's go somewhere else," Selene suggested to the Listener. "Somewhere to take our minds off all this carnage and avoid those storm clouds."

At Selene's request, our boat appeared off the coast of San Diego, California. There, we arrived in the early hours of the evening and witnessed such a spectacular sight. The waves that lapped the sandy shore were glowing a luminescent blue. It was more than enough to ease my troubled mood.

"Let's anchor the boat and relax on the beach. What an incredible thing to see!" I cheered happily.

Sitting on the beach, Selene and I gazed, mesmerised at the phosphorescent show whilst the Listener explored the coastline and knowingly gave us our space. Selene had transformed her beautiful tail into human legs, and I did my best to look 'human-like' again to not draw attention to ourselves. The beach was busy with people who were more interested in holding their phones up to the blue waves than interacting with a weird-looking humanoid such as me.

"I've always been a fan of phytoplankton. I think that the ones responsible for this light show are perhaps my favourite," I sighed gleefully with a wide grin on my face.

"I'm glad you are feeling so happy," Selene replied with a caring tone to her voice. "It's been a tough time for both you and the ocean."

"Look at these waves. Look at how magical the sea can be," I exclaimed. "After tonight, I will think about what I can do to protect the ocean."

"OK," Selene nodded in agreement. "But yes, let's enjoy ourselves."

"I have a gift I want to give you," I blushed bashfully. "Close your eyes and hold out your hands."

Selene cupped her soft, pink nail-painted hands and averted her gaze. I carefully placed a perfect pearl on her palms, making sure to protect her skin from my claws.

"Oh wow!" she cried, being brought to tears. "Thank you! Where did you get this from?"

"From a Japanese Ama lady," I revealed. "A human mermaid."

"It's beautiful," Selene beamed before embracing me. We kissed passionately as the vivid blue waves crashed before us, a moment that I will cherish forever.

"This time with you, enjoying the ocean has been one of the most magical times of my life. Even on dark days, you are the moonlight that shines through the storm clouds and lifts my spirits," I expressed. "I hope that you will always be with me and I hope we will continue to have more adventures. For now, this pearl is me saying, thank you for this incredible time."

Our wonderful moment was cut short by the sounds of shouting further down the beach. The Listener ran back to us and pointed towards a group of people who seemed to be beating or attacking something with sticks. We heard wails and grunts following the sounds of thuds and maniacal laughter.

"What in the world?!" I cried, feeling my pupils dilate and my body fill with adrenaline.

I jumped up and ran, albeit clumsily due to my large, webbed feet. My claws grew sharper with every moment that I heard the cries. The spikes on my back, shoulder and forehead also elongated and flared for me to seem more threatening, whilst tentacles re-grew in between my messy green hair. My teeth became more extensive and sinister, as I readied myself to bare them at whoever was harming what I thought they were hurting.

I hoped and prayed that what I was about to see was not real. I loved humanity, but when I saw that group of people beating a lone sea lion, I felt a rage I had never felt before. It was deeper than my anger towards the Island of the Fallen. I roared, I hissed, I swiped with my razor-sharp claws. My shoulders grew so large that I found myself transforming into something almost wolf-like. Amongst my already sharp teeth, canines grew, and I gnashed my jaws as I jumped towards the gang.

"What the...?!" cried one of the group. "What is this thing?!"

"I don't know! Run!" yelled another of them as he threw a stick to the ground. He almost tripped over himself when trying to run away as fast as possible.

The gang dispersed pretty much as soon as they saw me. I almost found myself unable to calm down and wanted so much to help the injured sea lion. Selene ran up to us and comforted the poor animal whilst I slowly transformed from mega-monster back to 'normal' monster.

Eventually, after some time giving the sea lion gentle strokes and making them feel safe, they let out a sigh of relief before waddling back towards their colony. We walked at a safe distance from them just to make sure they got back to their kind without any more attacks.

"I mean, why?" I gasped to Selene and the Listener as we travelled back towards the boat. "Were they hunting it for food? What was the purpose of that?"

"Humans have always harboured a cruel streak. Why are you so surprised? You have seen what humans do to each other throughout time. Of course, they are cruel to other species too," Selene replied in a matter-of-fact tone.

"Not all humans. I have witnessed great kindness and beauty from humanity," I reasoned, keeping in mind the time that I had spent with Yosef all those years ago.

"Look at what is happening to the ocean. Look at what is happening to you, Maddas,"

Selene warned. "I'm worried about what this anger is making you become. You turned into a different sort of creature back there."

"I didn't know what else to do," I replied. "All I knew was that I had to do something. I become whatever I need to be, depending on the situation. Maybe right now, I need to be a scarier monster, to reflect how monstrous humans are to my ocean home and all of its wonderful creatures."

"So, are you sad because Selene saw you transform into something stranger than you already are?" Viktor cut in as Maddas paused their story to sit up and come to terms with what had happened.

"It wasn't just that," Maddas continued.

"After that encounter, I needed to remind myself and show Selene that not all humans were a threat to the ocean. Some humans lived off and respected the seas. I wanted to show her the Ama, the Haenyeo and the Sama-Bajau. With storm clouds approaching us again, I directed the Listener to take us back to the oceans of East Asia, where I could introduce Selene to the human 'merfolk' that I had met.

Instead of arriving back at the seas near Japan, Jeju Island, or the Banda Sea, we overshot and arrived in the North Pacific Ocean. This time we were not at the 'Sea of Plastic' as before. We found an even more horrific sight.

We had ventured into a sea of still alive yet de-finned sharks. They had their means of swimming and breathing removed when onboard a fishing boat, then cast back to the sea, still bleeding, to then sink and drown.

I saw the humans aboard the boat, carrying out the abuse with their large nets and sharp knives. Without preparing much thought into what I was going to do about the situation, I dived into the sea. My salty tears merged with the ocean brine as dying sharks sank in the sea all around me.

The anger that I felt encompassed me. It became me. I was no longer a thinking being. The rage made me lose contact with the reality of the situation, so much that I don't necessarily remember what happened. What I'm telling you now is from what Selene said to me about what I did.

When I dived into the sea, a few moments passed before my anger radiated from my being into the surrounding waters. The blood-soaked sea began to turn into a funnel, with me at its centre. I had lost control of my emotions, and the result was the creation of a gigantic whirlpool. It sucked the shark finning boat into the fearsome watery centrifuge that I had created. In the process, however, the vortex also took the Listener's vessel, with Selene still on board. They cried out to me to stop, but I could not hear them.

The Listener dug into his record collection, throwing albums about the boat to find something that he knew would calm me. He needed to stop me before my whirlpool destroyed his cabin cruiser and everything else dear to me. He found an album that Yosef had recorded and played it.

The whirlpool died down as the tunes passed through to my wounded soul. I opened my eyes to see the destruction I was causing and tried to calm my breathing. I let myself float on the surface, wanting so much to rewind that moment.

"I'm sorry," I whimpered as the Listener dragged me into the boat. "I just... I don't know what is happening to me. I'm letting my anger take control of me. I feel like the rage is moving my body - it's like being a puppet controlled by mania."

"It's OK," Selene replied, looking at me with a worried expression."

"It wasn't OK," Maddas concluded to Viktor. "She watched as I became someone she didn't know. My anger turned me into an unrecognisable monster, not the usual monster she had come to appreciate."

"Crikey," Viktor exclaimed, listening to Patient Seven without any sign of judgement on his face.

"You listen to me so patiently Viktor," Maddas sobbed. "I don't deserve to meet little angels like you and Selene."

"I'm not that little," Viktor growled jokingly. "So, was that the reason why you are here?"

"...No," Maddas admitted. "There's more."

Purpose

"I'm here for a whole combination of things. When you feel attacked, angry, victimised, and helpless whilst also struggling to deal with the past, these things build up," Maddas explained to Viktor as they continued to spend time in the hallway. Maddas sat, hunched up on the bench whilst Viktor consoled them.

"I understand that," Viktor nodded empathetically.

"After the whirlpool incident, Selene and the Listener sat with me on the deck of the boat as we drifted around the North Pacific Ocean, trying to avoid the storm clouds that were following me again. They were both worried about me and but also their own safety.

"I know you still need to face the Island. You cannot wage war with humans over the ocean whilst still dealing with the trauma from your past. Only when you take a few steps back can you truly move forward," Selene reasoned with me. I gazed downwards at the wooden deck of the boat, wrecked by shame at what I had become.

The Listener, with his arms folded, nodded, and agreed with Selene.

"I think I'm supposed to protect the ocean, though. I have all these powers now, and I need to fight a greater cause than worry about my past. My past will always be there for me to deal with, but right *now,* the ocean is being attacked. I need to live in the present and do what I can to stop the humans from destroying my world," I answered. My speech was still affected by the adrenaline I felt after the whirlpool incident and after witnessing the shark-finning carnage.

"You should maybe take some time to relax your mind if you can. Whatever you do, you should try to regain your calm. If you cannot control your emotions, you will do more damage to the planet than good. And you might do more damage to us," Selene replied with tears falling from her eyes.

"I don't know what I must do," I mused. "I'm so sorry, Selene. I never meant to hurt you. I never meant to hurt the Listener. My soul is in so much turmoil."

"I know what can help," Selene smiled, summoning inner strength. "Let's go and swim with some sea otters."

That evening, Selene and I played hide and seek amidst a giant kelp forest with a group of mischievous sea otters. Their cuteness and curiosity lifted our spirits, and for a moment, I felt happy again. I hid behind some vegetation to watch from afar as a sea otter swam about Selene and enjoyed being petted by her, and I felt so lucky that I had met such a wonderful mermaid. I was also so fortunate to have had a friend in the Listener.

However, the crushing guilt that I felt from causing the whirlpool led me to the decision that I should swim away and deal with my troubles alone. I could not risk any more harm to Selene or the Listener, especially if I had to face the cursed Island of the Fallen. So, whilst Selene was distracted by the sea otters, I quietly swam away.

I swooped out of the kelp forest and dived downwards, determined to swim far away from Selene and out her view. After a few kicks of my powerful webbed feet, I found myself in an ocean desert. My journey took me to a shipwreck that I thought might be an excellent place to hide for a while. Whatever my reason for finding it, I could sense that something about the wreckage was drawing me closer to it.

The wreck was very different from most of the modern-ish shipwrecks that I had encountered. It bore the design of a Viking ship from centuries past but was entirely composed of a metal that was resistant to corrosion, possibly aluminium.

I swam to the hull of the ship, noticing that there was a shiny surface glistening there. On inspection, it seemed to be a large, oval-shaped mirror. I tried to touch it with my hand and found that it was not glass. My arm disappeared into whatever was on the other side of the oval. I followed my claw and my curiosity and swam through the 'doorway' into what seemed to be another world entirely.

On the 'other side', I found myself still on the hull of that metal ship. However, instead of being surrounded by the ocean, the boat was encircled by an arid desert of red sand with no sign of seawater.

"Oh no, where am I?" I cried, feeling panicked at the combination of intense heat and the absence of the sea.

An airship arrived beside the boat a few moments after I had emerged into this bizarre world. The airship was much like the wreck that I stood on; it was designed like a Viking warship and made of shiny metal. However, it was floating in the air.

"Aqua Maddas!" cheered a woman from the airship. "Welcome!"

"Where am I? Who are you?" I winced.

"It's better to ask 'when' not 'where'," she smirked, holding out her hand to help my dizzy, confused self onto the airship. "I welcome you to Earth, 100 million years from your current year."

"OK," I nodded worriedly, steadying myself.

The woman had light-brown skin and long, platinum-blonde hair tied up in plaits. She seemed to be the leader of a small crew of five other women, all wearing their blonde manes in long braids as well.

"What happened to all the water? When I found the shipwreck, it was around forty metres below the ocean surface," I questioned.

"That's why I, or we, brought you here for a talk," she began with a grave seriousness in her voice. "My name is Freya, by the way."

"OK, Freya, can you tell me where the ocean is?"

"Let's take a trip on my airship. I will show you where it is."

"Actually, I should probably get back to the ocean in my time. I'm feeling very dehydrated already," I remarked, cautious about joining a group of unfamiliar women on a mysterious journey in their airship.

"Unfortunately, this won't take long," Freya sighed.

We travelled around the globe in Freya's super-fast ship, gazing at deserts and dry canyons. There were no humans at all. Covered by sand were the remnants of human cities. The only plants thriving seemed to be the odd cactus and some dry weeds. There were no polar ice caps, no waterfalls, no clouds, and no ocean at all. I felt itchy with worry and yearned for the water.

"What happened to the ocean?" I whimpered. "Where are all the animals? Where have all the humans gone?"

"The ocean is no more apart from one small area of the world. The Earth is no longer able to sustain life and is now pretty much abandoned. The only human survivors of the great floods when the ice caps melted fought each other for food and shelter. Famine and disease killed many of them. The few who did remain packed themselves into spaceships and said goodbye," Freya told me. "We are only able to breathe due to a forcefield around our ship."

"Are you going to leave too?"

"Not by spaceships. Our technology is different, for we are time-travellers."

"OK," Maddas nodded, having a difficult time taking in all the information. "I see you're a fan of Viking ship designs?"

"Oh, that's because the first time-travellers were Vikings," Freya explained.

"Time-travelling? Time-travelling Vikings?" Maddas frowned. "Am I dreaming?"

"Look, the rule is, Vikings always get there first, no matter where or what it is. Who were the first ones to travel to Africa, America, and Asia from Europe? Vikings. The first ones to find portals to the Future? Also, the Vikings."

"Vikings always get there first," added one of Freya's crew.

"Although, you've already met one time-traveller. The ones descended from Vikings kept their time-travelling airships in keeping with traditional Viking warships. Other time-travellers disguise their time-jump devices as out-of-place machines, for example, record players that steer little boats."

"The Listener?"

"Exactly," nodded Freya. "Your quiet friend is a time-traveller. His quest was to help you realise your purpose on this planet. The reason for being Aqua Maddas entirely."

"That's fascinating. Can I ask, if the Listener is a time traveller, can he let me go back in time so that I can help some people I met in the past?

With my new powers, I may be able to do more to help those poor enslaved people in Jamaica. Or I could help Yosef survive the war? I could have helped a lot more people during those wars!" I cut in, excited by the prospect of time travel.

"Maybe you can do that at some point. But right now, your priority is to learn of your purpose," Freya replied sternly.

"Do I have a purpose?"

"Yes. You see, the Earth was already on course to dry up due to the increase in solar luminosity. However, due to humans causing climate change, the ocean dried up much earlier than predicted. Humans forgot how important protecting the ocean is. First, they used it as a dustbin, filling it full of pollutants and plastics. They also burnt fossil fuels so much that the ocean became too warm, and they did not see the signs of marine life becoming extinct. But those were not the worst things to happen."

"It's challenging preventing humans from destroying things," I commented, doing my best to suppress my anger.

"This is where you come in. If humans are to save themselves and their planet from an early demise, they must protect their ocean. They need not just to appreciate it; they need to *listen* to it. You see, Maddas, everything you are and everything you have become has led up to your reason for being on this planet. You are an Ocean Guardian, and you must protect that which helped to heal you, and which gave you a home," Freya instructed.

"How can I do this without destroying everyone I know and love. How can I do this without being a scary monster?"

"That might be what you need to be," Freya suggested. "But you have lived and breathed the music of humans. You have taken in their culture and lived through their histories with the Listener as your guide. You will know what it is that you must do."

The airship began to slow down and descend. It found a place to hover - above a small salt-lake with an Island at its centre.

"This is the only ocean left," Freya declared sadly. "But I wouldn't swim in it. It is a dead sea, and you will not find hydration there."

I gasped with horror at the ghost of the ocean, but also at what it surrounded.

"I think you might recognise the Island within it," she commented.

She was correct. My stomach sank as I became filled with overwhelming fear.

"The Island of the Fallen - YOUR Island, waits for you," Freya instructed. "There is a portal back to your time, but you must find it deep within the caves under the hill. Those caves will also reveal to you a secret about your existence. You will understand your reason for being here."

"I don't think I can do this alone," I winced.

"You're not alone. On the other side of the doorway, the Listener and Selene will be waiting for you. Go to the caves, and you will understand your place in this world."

"OK, Freya, I will do my best," I nodded, feeling my skin crawl. "So, this is how this happens. Island, I am back."

I jumped from the airship and landed onto the beach. The feeling of jagged stones underneath my webbed feet brought back a discomfort I thought I had forgotten for so many years. As I walked up towards the jungle, I took some deep breaths. In an Earth devoid of life, the Island of the Fallen's vegetation was still somehow thriving.

"Stay out of my way!" I yelled at 'the Grip' of the jungle. "If one vine so much as touches me, I will slash everything I see with one of my spears!"

As Maddas recalled what happened, they began to shake with adrenaline and become unsettlingly energetic.

"I think Maddas needs to take their meds," Viktor cut in to advise a Nurse passing by. The Nurse handed a little plastic pot of pills to Maddas, who took them before curling up and lying back down on the bench in the hallway.

"Maddas, you have been livelier than usual recently. We might have to increase the dose," the Nurse spoke with a nervous smile. Patient Seven met their expression with a thorny grin -

the pills tucked underneath their tongue as they pretended to swallow the medication.

The Island of the Fallen

The Nurse helped Maddas to stand up and led them to the Art Room in the hope of assisting Patient Seven to calm down. Viktor accompanied them, worried about the welfare of his new friend. Eventually, Susan, the Therapist, walked into the room and gestured for the others to leave but stand nearby just in case.

"Maddas, why are you more distressed than usual?" Susan asked. "What's happened?"

"I remember why I am here," Maddas began. "I remember the Reason I am here, in this place and this world."

"I remember walking warily across the beach of the Island of the Fallen. Voices travelled through the air as I approached the dreaded jungle. However, the words were softer and raspier than before, so it was difficult to understand their meaning.

As I strode through the jungle, my shoulders were tense and expansive - my spikes displayed prominently and sharper than usual. My body was ready to transform into something more feral or wolf-like if need be.

However, I noticed that the trees were black and grey and that fruits were falling from them and quickly decaying. The forest was dying. There were no more streams flowing down from the rocky hill - just dry ditches where the water once was. The voices became louder, and I began to understand what they were saying.

"You killed us, Aqua Maddas. It's all your fault," hissed the voices, echoing all around me. "You did this. You did not protect us. You did not stay. Now we are dying, and we are in a bad way," the voices sang. I remembered just how powerful and disturbing their hypnotic effect was.

I let out a roar, bared my teeth and decided to run on all fours. As I approached the rocky hill where the entrance of the cave was, I felt the presence of someone watching me. It was the stone Golem from many years ago. I glanced up to see that he was much smaller than I remembered him to be. With a snarl and a hiss from me, the Golem scuttled away and hid behind a large rock.

Despite it being millennia since I had seen the Island, I remembered its landscape as if I had never left. I was able to locate the cave entrance without much searching. However, I needed to lift massive boulders out of the way to climb into the cold darkness. I had forgotten the destruction I had caused to the cave the last time I had been there.

With an intense fear that I tried so hard to suppress; I clambered into the cave. I was shocked to see that the skeletal remains were still there, almost exactly as I had left them.

"So where is this portal?" I whispered to myself.

I stepped carefully around the pile of skeletons, trying my best not to crush any of them with my heavy, clawed feet. After examining my surroundings, I found that there was an entrance to another, much deeper cave. It was an opening that I had not noticed before.

Still hating the vulnerable situation that I had put myself in, I moved forward to explore.

My eyes adjusted themselves to the dark, as I travelled carefully along a narrow corridor. At one point, I even had to crawl on all fours as the cave ceiling got too low. My instincts told me that none of this felt right. I was feeling squeezed and squashed by the very place that I had been swimming from for my entire life.

At the end of the tunnel, I found an underground chamber, lit suddenly by blue, luminescent lamps. The portal back to my original time was in the centre of the cavity. I wanted so much to jump through it, run away from the Island and escape it all. However, I decided to investigate my surroundings.

Beside the portal was a large, pill-shaped capsule, about the size of a giant tortoise. Fascinating paintings decorated the cave walls, most of them coloured dark blue and cyan. There, the artwork depicted a spaceship coming to Earth, looking like a shooting star.

One picture showed blue beings wearing cloaks, filling the capsule with water, algae, seeds, and frogspawn-like eggs. Another image showed creatures that looked like me, hatching from those eggs. An incredible mural portrayed the cloaked beings placing the capsule in a round spaceship and then piloting the vessel towards an ocean planet.

Similar paintings were displayed all around the chamber, except that they showed different oceanic planets. One, I recognised as Earth from music-album artwork, but there were other blue planets. Some globes looked like Earth, but there with others with no landmass, and some covered with ice.

In most of the paintings, the ocean planets had arrows pointing to other worlds, except those were devoid of water. It seemed as though the pictures were expressing the message that watery planets would become completely dry, just as Freya had warned me.

Above and below the arrows were paintings of various animals. They were intriguing to me because I had not seen a few of them come into existence yet. I recognised jellyfish, swans, whales, and sharks, but I had never encountered human-sized rats, sharks with the legs of wolves or octopuses with hands.

"Are these the types of creatures to evolve and warn us of a changing planet?" I pondered to myself.

I was overwhelmed by the enormous amount of information presented to me through the artwork. It dawned on me that the skeletons in the cave were not those of humans. The remains were of the beings who brought the capsule to Earth. Perhaps they were trying to protect the key to life itself - the first 'eggs'?

Whoever they were, they had sacrificed everything to bring me here. There was one painting of the Island itself. A green, spiky being, perhaps me, was shown to hover above the Island, possibly guarding it. Above that picture was written 'Aqua Maddas - of the Ocean Planet Cycle'.

The voice of the Island reached me, echoing through the caves.

"This is your future, your destiny. You must protect us and save the sea."

I realised that the wall of the chamber was not stone - it was of some kind of metal composite. As well as the capsule, the 'metal cave' also housed a record player, very similar to the Listener's device. Beside the machine were just one album and a note. The album was the 'Aqua Maddas' album, with all the songs that had been played by the Listener during our adventures.

The note read:

'Please save this planet Earth. But if you cannot, and you need to escape, please accept this epic soundtrack for your journey. Best wishes, the Listener.'

I will admit, there was a moment that I looked around what I realised was a buried spaceship and strongly considered using it to leave Earth. I had spent my life running away from the Island of the Fallen and escaping from tricky situations on Earth. After feeling so angry with the humans and so ashamed about my harmful behaviour towards Selene and the Listener, I could feel the pull from my robust 'flight' response. However, my gaze turned towards the sparkling oval portal that I hoped would take me back to Selene's time.

"I will go back, and I will fight," I decided as I stepped determinedly through the gateway.

I arrived in the same place, in the same underground 'ship', but I noticed that some of the artwork was missing - notably the picture of the Island with me hovering above it. The voice of the Island found me again; this time, it was more coherent and full of vigour.

"You're back. I knew you would be back. Are you here to protect or are you here to attack?" the voice sang.

I let out another roar, which turned into a screech and hurried to get out of the underground system. I had no idea if I would be strong enough to break my way out if my surroundings caved in. I ran past the skeletons but stopped briefly to gaze admiringly at them.

"Thank you for all that you have done for me," I spoke solemnly. "I appreciate being here and the sacrifices you made for me."

"Stay with us for a while; we miss your wit; we miss your smile. For although we have died, our souls remain tied, to every cell, to every plant, to every stone. We are always with you, and you are not alone. Planets may die, and so will we, but we can protect the seeds of the sea. This is the voice of the Island of the Fallen - we

protect the secrets that fell through the sky. Now you must protect us, and this planet, and now you know why," the Island sang.

"I don't know what I should do," I winced. Tears fell from my eyes as they adjusted to the dazzling sunlight that met me as I stomped outside the cave. It was such a relief to see the light again after being in the eerie darkness.

"Remember who you are, you're from an egg in a little shooting star," sang the voice.

Honestly, I was looking forward to never hearing that voice again - it gripped every nerve in my body, every cell, and every strand of DNA - if I carried any at all.

Taking deep breaths, I looked at the jungle and its writhing vines, all primed to lunge towards me and grab my arms, wrists, leg, or face. No sense in my body told me that I was safe.

"The Grip, do you hear me? Let me through!" I bellowed powerfully, raising my sharp, serrated claws threateningly. I prepared myself to lurch back into 'feral' mode.

The forest suddenly parted. Vines had receded and made a clear pathway through the rainforest. I stamped through it, making my way to the small river - the place where I first emerged from, after my tadpole stage. I was so relieved to see water still trickling down from the hilltop. There were still reeds and frogs and tiny minnows hiding in the brook.

I paused to look at my reflection in the water and take in how much I had changed since my cave-dwelling days. That moment, I think, is one of the reasons why I am here in this place."

"How do you mean?" asked the Therapist.

"When I checked my reflection," Maddas began, "I was no longer spiky, with my sharp teeth, gills, tentacle hair and claws. The creature staring back at me was a tiny, pink-green blob-like thing that stared back at me with terrified eyes. They were soft, vulnerable, weak, and unprepared for a world that would eventually turn them into a monster. The person looking back at me was not Aqua Maddas. They were Small."

My Message

"How did that make you feel, Maddas?" Susan, the Therapist, probed.

"Feel?" Maddas snapped. "I don't remember feeling anything!"

Susan and Maddas were in the Art Room, surrounded by an extraordinary amount of Maddas's sketches. They were of different aquatic animals, the fate of the planet and maps of the Island of the Fallen.

"But I feel calmer when I draw," Maddas mentioned, with a voice betraying extreme agitation. As they spoke to Susan, they doodled more pictures.

"Can you tell me what happened on the Island?" Susan asked.

"Everything about the Island that I had tried to escape, rushed into my being and engulfed me. The gaze of the Golem, the terror of the caves, the fear from the sinking sand and grasping vines. Then finally, the hypnotic but chilling voice that emanated from the Island. I felt as though all of it became absorbed into my mind," Maddas explained.

"I screamed and held my claws up to the sky in a desperate cry for help. Storm clouds appeared above me, conjured by my disturbed and furious mental state. My entire body was no longer 'mine'. Something else, perhaps the spirits of the Island, controlled my being. My body levitated above the land and into the clouds. Whilst I hovered in the sky, my incorporeal self separated from me. In fact, at one point, though my detached consciousness, I was able to see my own body floating.

The oceans surrounding the Island became violent and destructive. The water rose and encircled the Island whilst the storms above turned into a terrifying tornado that merged with a watery maelstrom below. The Island, with me hovering above the centre of it, became the eye of an impenetrable storm.

My incorporeal self drifted away from me and became at one with the storm clouds. However, it did not stop at that. My soul merged with rain tumbling to the ground. I had connected to the flowing rivers and streams that linked the Island with the ocean, and not just the sea nearby. I felt as though I was in every part of the brine, in every area of the world.

My essence was in the clouds hanging over every landmass. I was the water vapour in the air, able to reach every living thing on the planet. My consciousness connected to the water flowing through blood vessels of every human. I had access to the water held in every human cell. Although I had left my body and felt as though I had become 'nothing' and 'nowhere', I was everywhere, and my thoughts were able to reach everyone. I could affect every human mind and manipulate their thoughts.

People all over the world suddenly perceived that their cities had transformed into kelp forests, with seals and fish winding their way through alleyways. I made people think that parks and gardens had become coral reefs, teeming with colourful little fishes and layers of psychedelic sponges and anemones. Anyone inside thought that shoals of small fishes flowed in through windows. Even people in prisons, hospitals and schools saw octopuses, jellyfish and eels enter their domains. My voice was able to enter the minds of every human alive.

"Even if you cannot swim or get to the ocean, I will share with you its beauty. You must protect it with everything you have, just as you must protect your planet. Sure, there may be other worlds to go to when the seas dry up, but you will make the same mistakes over and over again unless you learn to appreciate what you have right now. The animals of this planet, everything that has ever evolved - came from the sea. Stop dumping your plastic, stop polluting it and stop driving its creatures to extinction!" I boomed to every human soul.

An image of myself appeared to any person that could see. For anyone blind, I filled their senses with the texture of my scaly skin and spikes.

"If the thought of having to leave your planet earlier than expected does not scare you, the events leading up to it should do," I continued to barrage. "The predators of the sea will be introduced to your islands with every moment that your ocean levels rise. As the polar ice caps melt, the sharks and ray fish will evolve as every creature does. Their fins will turn into legs, and they will begin to roam your landmasses. They will be ruthless apex predators, more bone-chilling than the fiercest tigers, wolves and bears."

I made everyone hallucinate the horrors of a world with sharks able to travel on land with the agility and determination that they display in the ocean. People started to panic as they began to see landscapes full of ray fish crawling around, lying in wait to sting or electrocute their prey.

"Then, the land will become too hot. The ocean will be too warm. The sea will start to evaporate until every part of it becomes the Dead Sea. Maybe some of your descendants will escape and find another planet if they should survive famine, disease, and starvation. I am Aqua Maddas, and this is my message. Protect my Sea, or you will not escape me."

After I let go of humanity's psyche, I let my incorporeal mind roam to a few places. I needed to connect with the humans that were friends of the ocean, and who wanted to help in whatever way they could.

To the beautiful souls picking up litter on the beaches, to the enterprising heroes clearing plastic from the oceans, to the diligent scientists monitoring the climate and biodiversity, and to the activists yelling out for humanity to change its ways, my incorporeal self appeared to them and swooned 'I see you, and I thank you'. I blew them a kiss which made them feel as though a little shoal of fish passed them through the air.

Then finally, my essence hung around in a small cemetery. It was a secret resting place, locked to the public. High gates and foreboding brick walls with barbed wire protected weathered gravestones. There, I found his grave — the grave of Yosef.

"Your last name is Zaderikhvost?" I commented. "I didn't know that until now."

His grave read 'fallen in battle', written in Hebrew. With much concentration, my incorporeal self was strong enough to pick up a small stone and place it respectfully on his grave.

Immediately after, I found myself back in my physical being. I was still levitating, but I had sunk back almost to ground level. Someone had been able to get through the harsh tornado winds and the chilling maelstrom — someone with soft, warm, but firm hands. Selene had broken through and had braved the Island of the Fallen to 'ground' me.

"I think it's time for you to get some help, Maddas," Selene spoke to me softly."

"And that is why I am here," Patient Seven concluded to the Therapist.

"I'm sorry, what were you saying about sharks...evolving legs?" Susan winced. "That's such a scary thought. I have a phobia of sharks."

"It *should* scare you," Maddas replied solemnly.

"I've noticed that you've been doing a lot of drawing lately," Susan commented as she glanced at the ever-growing pile of sketches in front of Maddas. "Are they of the creatures that you say will evolve?"

"Welcome to my 'Art-Quarium'," Maddas grinned. "You will find many creatures here. Some of them are scary; some of them are weird. But they all have something in common.

They are all just trying to survive in an ever-changing world. As am I."

"Medication!" yelled one of the Nurses entering the Art Room abruptly.

"No!" Maddas yelled back. "I will only take your pills if you take the medicine that *I'm* trying to give you! You need to listen to me!"

Patient Seven suddenly stood up, flaring their shoulders aggressively.

"Please Maddas, you need to take this."

"I am not the one who is mad," Maddas growled. "I shouldn't be in here! I should be swimming in the ocean! I should be protecting my seas! My world!"

"Please Maddas, you need to go to your room and take your pills," the Nurse pleaded, trying to get close to Patient Seven. Susan, the Therapist, vacated the room swiftly.

"I didn't want to have to do this, but you leave me with no choice!" Maddas screamed. "I have no choice!"

Nothing You Can Do

Selene sat with a tense posture in the Doctor's office, accompanied by Susan, the Therapist. Susan offered Selene a cup of tea and some tissues, but they did not provide much comfort. Her legs shook with anxiety.

"Has there been any improvement at all?" Selene asked.

"I'm sorry to say, Selene, your partner is still under the belief that they are a sea creature called Aqua Maddas or an alien from outer space. They still have psychosis," the Therapist informed. "Their symptoms have been worse than usual in the last couple of days."

"They seem to be refusing to take the medication, as well as pretending to take it when appearing to comply," the Doctor added.

"They were not happy to take the medication when I offered it to them," Selene nodded. "Are they sleeping at all?"

"It seems so at times, but not very much," the Therapist answered.

"Do you think they will recover?" Selene sobbed.

"It's hard to say at this moment. If they take the antipsychotic medication and the sedatives, and eat and sleep normally then they will recover," the Doctor advised. "Right now, it's difficult to say when that will happen, if ever."

"Is there anything I can do?" Selene asked, wiping her tears with the tissues.

"I'm sorry. There is nothing that you can do. Perhaps when you speak to them, mention the importance of the medication," Susan suggested. "But I would recommend not seeing them right now. They are more 'energetic' than usual and could be dangerous."

The alarm suddenly pierced through the unit. Several Nurses rushed to the Art Room to try to sedate an aggressive Maddas. Patient Seven stood on the Art Room table and had armed themselves with a chair. Viktor was also nearby, trying to coax them down.

Maddas caught sight of Selene through the window of the Art Room door. They jumped off the table in an attempt to get to her, but several

Nurses restrained them. Maddas cried out as Selene walked away to escape the unit and get some fresh air.

Section 2

Patient Seven wrestled themselves free from the Nurses restraining them. They ran out of the Art Room and sprinted through the communal area to get to the yard outside. They jumped onto the tennis table and pointed their claws towards the storm clouds hanging above the hospital. Nurses were trying their best to coax Maddas down but were interrupted by the sound of another alarm.

In the communal area, Jeff had suddenly held up a kitchen knife to Viktor who began to fight him in self-defence. The Nurses left the yard to respond to yet another chaotic situation.

"Perfect," Maddas grinned. "If I can't make you love the ocean, I will bring it here, for real this time."

They clapped their claws together and danced clumsily on the table as rain poured down from the thick clouds above. Water rapidly filled the yard, and Maddas was elated to wade through a newly formed mini 'sea'. Aquatic animals fell from the sky, to inhabit the environment.

Patient Seven opened the door to the unit, letting the water gush into the communal area. Amidst cries from Nurses and Doctors telling Maddas to take their medication, Patient Seven surrounded themselves with a mini whirlpool as the water levels rose to engulf the unit.

The whole place became akin to an aquarium. Patient Seven's artwork of strange future creatures swirled in another whirlpool inside the Art Room. Eels, turtles, and small sharks joined the sketches from Maddas's makeshift 'ocean'. The medical staff and most of the other patients escaped the area as Maddas swam through the unit.

Patient Seven embraced the freedom of somersaults and drifted effortlessly through the water. Viktor grinned as he joined Maddas in enjoying swimming about the new aquatic environment.

Magenta tentacles re-grew from in between Maddas's green hair. The extra appendages danced on their own accord, sometimes grabbing and throwing chairs about so that fast-growing coral could become the dominant feature of the communal area. Maddas grabbed biscuits from the breakfast area and crushed them, throwing their crumbs to the eye-catching sea carp that hoovered them up without much hesitance.

Shoals of glassfish and impressive groupers swam past as Maddas made their way to the corridor near their dormitory room. The passage had also been transformed into a sea life 'tank', as ray fish, crabs and lobsters crawled on the sandy ground whilst gigantic sunfish swam slowly about. Maddas opened the corridor door with one of their tentacles and entered it, becoming aware of the door shutting and locking behind them.

There, they drifted from one end of the corridor to the other, looking into the different rooms of the other patients. These rooms were not filled with water like the rest of the unit. When Maddas peered through the windows of their doors, they noticed that some of the characters sitting in their rooms looked familiar to them.

The Listener sat in Room One, enjoying music from a record player atop their bedside table. He waved at Maddas through his dormitory room window. In Room Two sat the 'human-like' version of Maddas, the one that clung to the memory of Yosef. In Room Three was the Maddas with tentacle hair, crying to themselves about their terrifying appearance and clingy behaviour. In Room Four, there sat the Maddas that had disappeared to the bottom of the ocean. They were sitting in the dark, enjoying the bioluminescence from their translucent body.

In Room Five, there was the 'sea witch' version of Maddas, proud to embody fierce femininity. Room Six held the feral version of Maddas. They stomped around their room on all fours, ready to attack anything that seemed to be a threat.

Finally, in Room Seven sat the being that Maddas had feared the most. Patient Seven glanced through the door window, terrified of the shivering, vulnerable being that had been waiting for them for what seemed like millennia.

"Can I come in?" Maddas asked them.

Slowly and calmly, Small opened the door of their dormitory room and let Aqua Maddas in from the watery corridor. The room was dry-ish, although Maddas brought some of the ocean with them in the form of droplets and reeds.

"Take a seat," Small uttered, offering a space beside them on the bed.

"Sure," Maddas smiled.

"Do you remember me?" Small began.

"Of course. I was you for some time," Maddas nodded, their eyes attempting to suppress tears.

"You are *still* me," Small gulped, also beginning to sob.

"I am NOT you," Maddas growled. "I am the fearsome Aqua Maddas, Guardian of the Ocean and the Island of the Fallen! I am a supernatural being from outer space, and my purpose is to save the ocean and the planet! I am scary, strong, and spiky. People fear me!"

"I know, Maddas, I know," Small nodded with empathy as they stroked Maddas's scaly, spiky arm. Small's soft, gelatinous hands were a stark contrast from Maddas's scales and spines.

"I know YOU fear me," Maddas threatened.

"From the sharp claws to the tentacles in your hair, you have helped me overcome so much," Small mused. "But we're not from an Island of the Fallen, are we Maddas?"

"We're from an Island protected by beings who fell to earth from outer space!" Maddas shouted.

"It's time to really explore that Island," Small carried on. "The violence of the earth tremors, those were their fists and feet. The Grip of the forests and the pull of the sinking sand, those were fingers and hands taking advantage of our vulnerability. The Golem was the person ordering me to accept my fate. The hypnotic voice that sang through the wind - that was their way to brainwash you and convince you that things were harmonious. That was their way to lull you into a false sense of comfort."

"Stop," Maddas cried.

"You, or we, sought comfort in the ocean because that was the only place we felt safe. The people who chased us feared the unpredictability of the ocean. However, you understood it because you had mastered the art of surviving in an unpredictable environment. And, when you had to leave the ocean, you never let it go. You kept it in your mind and clung to its comfort, like the crabs that wouldn't let go of your hands when you played with them in the sea," Small continued.

"The ocean is my home! The ocean is me!" Maddas yelled desperately as their webbed feet started to melt slowly into a puddle of water on the floor.

"Thank you for healing me, and for helping me to escape when I needed to. But it is time to stop evolving. It is time to go back. It's time to be me," Small stated assertively.

"You are me!" cried Maddas as their legs also transformed into water and merged with the puddle.

"And you are me," Small replied calmly as they watched Maddas's scales and spines slowly become water droplets. "It's time for you to leave my mind."

Small choked back tears as they caught the saline streams gushing from Maddas's eyes.

"You can't let me go! I will always be with you!" Maddas yelled, before their scaly face disappeared and faded into the puddle.

"I will never forget you Aqua Maddas," Small lamented as Maddas's forehead horns and green hair evaporated.

"Don't let go of me!" Maddas shouted one final time.

"You must let go of me," Small retorted, staring into Maddas's eyes as their scaly face vanished.

A tentacle from Maddas's disappeared head reached out to grab Small's soft, fleshy hand before it too disintegrated into the aquatic puddle below.

Patient Seven sighed as they sat quietly on their bed and looked out of the door's window. The corridor was bone dry, with Nurses walking about in response to another alarm. Feeling cold for the first time in a long time, they wrapped themselves in a grey, fluffy jacket and looked to the piece of paper on their bedside table.

'You are being kept in this hospital under Section 2 of the Mental Health Act 1983. You have been examined by two Doctors, and they think that you have a mental disorder...' said the letter. Patient Seven checked 'Part 1' of the message, which revealed the Patient's Name.

"My name is Max?" they frowned with confusion before truly understanding the gravity of their situation. "I am Max, not Maddas?"

Once it had dawned on them that they were a human being, locked in a mental health hospital, they collapsed backwards onto their bed.

"Oh, my f*****g cr*ap!" they cried.

Wake Up

Max gazed at themselves in their dormitory wash-room mirror for about an hour. They were astonished at their soft skin, human hair, and lack of gills. There were no spikes present, just some scars on their back and arms from mysterious origins.

They splashed their face with water before using the toothbrush from a vanity kit. On glancing at their reflection again, they saw for a few moments a green-blue creature with tentacle hair, sharp teeth, gills, and cyan eyes. After a couple of blinks, their reflection returned to that of their usual human self.

At the breakfast area, Max concentrated on one task at a time. For once, they were able to savour the flavours of warm toast with jam. The Nurse Agwe joined them and expected Max to talk more.

"Don't you have a story for me, Maddas?" Agwe asked with a beaming smile.

"My name is Max," was the reply. "I have nothing to say."

"This is very different behaviour from you," Agwe remarked, scratching his head.

"Did you get your pay Agwe?" Max asked, recalling some details from an earlier conversation.

"Yes! Yes, I did in the end, but after many arguments," Agwe replied, his eyes wide with joy. "You remembered that? I think your mind is healing, Max!"

Max looked towards the TV on the wall that overlooked the communal space. They were happy to see that the news focussed on recent efforts to clear plastic from the oceans and clean up litter from beaches.

"And look at that Max, people do care about the ocean. You went on about it so much, it seems as though someone was Listening to you!" laughed Agwe as he patted Max's shoulder.

Max was so shocked about what Agwe had said that they accidentally spilt a glass of water on themselves. Agwe gave Max some kitchen paper to pat down the liquid.

Max looked down at their body to see that beneath their clothes, their skin had bluish-green scales. Their feet were long, webbed and had toes with sharp claws. They jumped out of their chair, spilling more water, and causing some disturbance in the area. Some of the other patients looked at Max with confusion.

"It might be time for your medication," Agwe stated as he calmly helped Max relax back into their seat.

Max looked down at their body to see that they were wearing a fluffy, grey jacket, green cargo shorts and some sandals. Their skin was still pink, and their feet were normal, with no webbing or spiked claws. However, their toenails could have done with a thorough trim.

A young man sat next to the puzzled Max. He had a minimal breakfast of one cup of tea and no solid food.

"Morning, Maddas," he greeted.

"It's Max. Who are you?" Max squinted, trying to work out who the young man was. For a couple of seconds, Max saw that the man had transformed into a Seahorse-type creature before changing back into a normal human being. He wore glasses, had slightly pale skin, and was wearing a dark-blue hooded jacket.

"You know me, it's Viktor remember?" the young man laughed, smirking at Max's perceived forgetfulness.

"You're not a seahorse," Max observed.

"What?" frowned Viktor.

"I think I need to get some more sleep," Max muttered, finding that hanging onto reality was incredibly exhausting.

"You're finally sleeping!" Agwe exclaimed happily. "Viktor, this is a good day for Max. It is probably a good day for all of us. I mean, we liked your stories, but we were wondering when you were going to 'wake up'."

Max stared into space, processing what Agwe had said. It was true; Max did feel as though they had woken up from a long dream but without any well-rested feeling.

"It's probably a good idea for you to go back to your room," Viktor advised. "I heard that Jeff was looking for you. Agwe, something needs to be done about Jeff. He's violent."

"We are keeping an eye, don't worry," Agwe assured Viktor.

After wilfully taking their medication, Max spent the remainder of the day locked in their dormitory room, by themselves. They leafed through all the history and nature books and magazines they had hoarded beside their bed. Perhaps they hoped it would inspire some hallucinations. However, Max became very aware that they were now in the 'real' world. They could no longer hide behind books and become lost in delusions and daydreams. It was time to face the good and bad of being a human.

"Being human is not all bad, I guess" Max mumbled to themselves as they ate some of the biscuits that Selene had brought them.

Later that night, they were happy to feel sleepy for once in a long time. They lay down on their dormitory bed, letting their medication-driven drowsiness take hold. Before closing their eyes, they gazed at the ceiling. In a flash, they saw a being hovering above them that they recognised as Aqua Maddas, a comic book character they had once created.

"Aqua Maddas," Max mumbled. "I remember now; I made you. You were a character I was going to put into a cartoon. I was going to make you go viral online to raise awareness about the ocean and climate change."

"Do you remember why?" Maddas replied, their voice was hollow but melodic in some way.

"I was depressed. I was so depressed about what happened to me as a child, and I was suffering from complex PTSD. When Sertraline did not help me, I tried to self-medicate by learning to freedive. I wanted to escape from my troubles on land, and enjoy an alien world underneath the waves," I spoke to myself, processing my memories.

"Do you remember creating me?" Maddas asked me.

"Yes. When I explored the ocean and blogged about it, I became acutely aware of how much it is under threat from humanity. I channelled my inner rage into creativity and wanted to do something about the abuse of the ocean. Whilst I could do nothing to save myself from my past, I felt I could do something about the present. I created a cartoon character, Aqua Maddas, intending to entertain and inspire people to love and protect the ocean and other blue spaces."

"I am not just a 'character', Max. I *am* you. Let me back in. We can do great things together," Maddas ordered, attempting to gain control of Max's mind once more.

"I am NOT you. You are NOT me," Max shouted as they turned to the side and closed their eyes. One of the Nurses arrived at Patient Seven's door to check on Max, who was trying so hard to ignore the green-blue being that hovered above them as they tried to sleep.

Dolphin?

Max was reading in their dormitory room when one of the Nurses arrived and told them that they had a couple of visitors. Max quickly checked the mirror to make sure they were still human and looked more presentable than usual, before scuttling to the communal area. There they saw two of their best friends from what seemed like many lifetimes ago.

"Max!" a young man with curly blonde hair cried. "It's so good to see you looking better!"

"Ben? Benedict?" Max exclaimed, making sure to say the correct name whilst hugging their friend.

"What on earth happened to you?" asked Max's other friend, a well-dressed young Cantonese man.

"Yi, I honestly don't know," Max muttered. "Tea?"

Max clumsily worked out how to make some tea for their friends in the kitchen corner of the communal area as Benedict and Yi sat down. Max's friends examined the hospital ward with eyes wide with curiosity.

"Um, I'm sorry if I scared you both or said some bizarre stuff," Max murmured sheepishly. "It felt as though I had been 'visited' by a disturbed creature who took hold of my mind. I heard them chattering in my brain, telling me to say and do certain things. My 'purpose' was to stop humans from mistreating the ocean."

"I remember that you wrote your blog as if you were an aquatic being," recalled Yi.

"I recall Selene being beside me at one point. Then I think I was escorted into a white van, possibly an ambulance. Nurses strapped me to a seat and watched over me. The next moment, I wake up from a dreamlike state and realise that I am here," Max explained.

"The main thing is that you're getting better," Benedict remarked, sipping the tea cautiously.

"Yes, I do feel so much better," Max replied shakily. "Do you know how long I've been here?"

"It's been about three weeks I think," Benedict informed.

"So, what have I missed?" Max asked.

As Yi and Benedict updated Max on what had been happening outside the ward, Max gave the impression that they were listening intently. However, they became distracted. As Benedict spoke, Max's mind perceived his face as becoming longer, his hair disappearing and his body developing rubbery skin and fins. To Max, Benedict had transformed into a half-dolphin, half-man creature.

"You're a dolphin, though. Shouldn't you get back to the sea?" Max cut in, interrupting Benedict's words.

"Pardon?" Benedict frowned.

"Oh, sorry. I must have been daydreaming for a second," Max spluttered, shocked at what their mind was capable of conjuring.

"Um, we brought you some ginger biscuits," Yi grinned, changing the subject.

Max and his friends chatted for a while before they were interrupted by another patient who started yelling. Amidst the usual chaos of the mental health ward, Yi and Benedict decided it was time for them to leave. They embraced in a group hug before leaving Max to their life in the hospital.

"Did Max just call you a dolphin?" Yi muttered to Benedict as they walked away.

"Thank you for visiting me!" Max called to them before sitting back down in the communal area with their arms around them, as if in a self-hug.

"I bet everyone on the outside sees me as this disturbed, mad person," they shuddered to themselves. "Is that who I am now? After everything I have achieved in my life, is this my fate?"

Max slumped back to their dormitory but was called again to the communal area by a Nurse.

"Maddas, or Max? You have another visitor!" the Nurse cried. "You're popular today!"

Max was mostly happy about the number of visitors but also filled with fear and distress. They had become aware of where they were and how they looked to those visiting from the outside world. They were afraid of being judged, examined, and perhaps ridiculed.

There in the communal area was a woman with longish brown hair and glasses, wearing a beautiful floral dress. She greeted Max with a warm smile and a long, tight hug.

"Max!" she exclaimed. "I brought you some flowers."

"Oh, that's so kind of you, Sam," Max grinned, holding back tears of gratitude. "Thank you for coming to see me."

"No problem at all," she replied cordially.

"You don't seem to be too bothered about being here," Max added, readying themselves to make more cups of tea.

"Something similar happened to another friend of mine. It is not so unusual. It's just that no one talks about it," Sam reasoned while helping Max make the tea. "I know you like biscuits as well. I brought you some."

"Can't say no to that," Max grinned. "And yes, I agree, no one does talk about psychosis, mania and delusions. When I get outside, I hope that maybe I can raise awareness and start some difficult conversations. That's after I finish my ocean awareness blog and cartoon."

"You still have a billion projects on the go at any one time," Sam laughed. "Maybe when you get outside you can learn to relax a little bit."

"Never," Max chuckled.

"I've always been a big supporter of your climate change and ocean awareness blogs, though, Max. I still think you should bring that Aqua Maddas cartoon character to life," Sam suggested.

"Thank you," Max shuddered, feeling watched by the ghostly figure of an aquatic being that followed them everywhere. "Perhaps we could go outside for a little bit? I know you like gardens. I can show you around the garden here. I planted something there, I think."

"Yes! Let's take the tea outside!" Sam exclaimed.

They both left the communal area for the outside yard. Sam's long dress trailed behind them, sometimes sweeping up debris from the ground. Max introduced their friend to the tennis table, some benches, and the little patch of soil where they had planted some strawberry seedlings not too long ago.

Sam spoke to Max about their garden and all the work they had put into making it a magical place. As Sam chatted, Max started to daydream again. This time, Max envisioned that roots from the ground reached Sam's feet. They saw Sam as being connected to nature and the earth through these roots. Max shook their head abruptly, jolting themselves out of their vision.

"Are you OK, Max?" Sam asked.

"Please don't judge me," Max whimpered. "I am finding it hard to stay in reality. I don't know why I have psychosis or what the point of it is. I just know that I will never be the same again or seen in the same way again by others."

"I'm not an expert on psychiatric medicine, Max," Sam began. "But it is not something that you could ever control, and it's not something that you should be ashamed of. You have been through a great deal in the past. With your history, it is no wonder that you lost your mind. It may have even been a coping mechanism to help you deal with some difficult issues."

"That might be true," Max pondered. "Before I came here, I remember now. I faced the people who abused me when I was a child. Before confronting them, I dealt with my memories and feelings by pushing them to the back of my mind. I put them all in a lost 'Island', surrounded by an ocean that comforted me. When I faced my fears, my mind became something else for a little bit. I thought I was the sea creature, Aqua Maddas. It gave me a sense of strength and meaning."

"That character was something you created. It came from your soul and may have been a part of you wanting to reach out. Even though you feel like you were someone else, perhaps you were becoming more yourself than you thought?" Sam debated. "Honestly, I don't know. I am not an expert. Just know that you are not alone with this. Some people may treat you differently after this experience, but I will be there for you."

"Thank you. You're a good friend," Max sobbed, hugging Sam tightly.

Suddenly Jeff emerged from the communal area into the yard. He was holding a sharp kitchen knife and was running straight towards Max, who swerved to get out of Jeff's way.

"Get back inside!" Max cried out to Sam as they both ran around the garden, trying to avoid Jeff. Max looked towards the window of the communal area and saw that Selene was there, watching in horror. As Jeff lunged towards Max, intending to stab them, Max jumped away and ran with Sam, back inside and joined Selene.

Max gazed out of the window to watch Jeff. The disturbed man was slicing the air with the knife. For a moment, Max saw that Jeff's target was the translucent green-blue figure of Aqua Maddas. The being seemed to wink at Max before disappearing.

"Jeff can see Aqua Maddas!" Max exclaimed to Sam and Selene who exchanged worried glances with each other.

You Are Certainly Not Alone

A couple of years after their recovery, Max received an invitation to tell their story at a virtual Recovery Conference held online, that had been organised by PATH, NHS. They switched on their laptop, calmed themselves and rehearsed their words before an introduction by the chairwoman. To add to the pressure, they were observing a religious fast that day. The hunger certainly affected their ability to control their nerves.

A few moments preceding their talk, Max received a message of encouragement from Michelle, one of their mental health support workers.

"You can do it!" read the message. Max smiled and remembered all the kind, helpful words that Michelle and all the other PATH workers had spoken to them.

"...And now, Max Coster will present to us 'Life After Psychosis'. Go ahead, Max!" bellowed the chairwoman.

"Hi All," Max began. They hoped with all their might that Aqua Maddas would not 'visit' them during their talk.

"Everyone has a different story when it comes to mental health. I find that I am met with some sympathy when I talk about suffering from depression and anxiety. However, when I speak about mania, psychosis, and hearing voices, I usually get shut down. People do not know how to talk about it. Some people get scared or have no idea how to relate. I hope that by sharing my story, perhaps it will help to encourage healthy dialogue around the subject.

By day I am a Scientist, specialising in biology. When I am not involved in drug discovery, I swim, freedive, snorkel, paint aquatic animals and blog about the ocean. My favourite pastime is exploring and enjoying the sea, lakes, and rivers. They are my 'safe spaces'. I had a troubled family history, and my way to escape was to imagine I was swimming in the ocean. I am also someone who binges on nature documentaries about aquatic environments.

Additionally, I am also interested in history, geography, and human rights. If I am not thinking about the sea, I will get lost in reading books and block out the world. In all honesty, I was always swimming away from the memories that haunted me. Those suppressed memories caused me to suffer from complex PTSD.

Annoyed that PTSD was taking over my life, I decided to confront the people who had caused it. A mixture of that and being on the wrong medication led my mind to 'break' in some way. I tried to use art and creative writing as a form of self-care and created a cartoon character called 'Aqua Maddas' - an aquatic humanoid who would roam the sea, try to solve the world's problems and raise awareness of ocean pollution. The name is derived from 'Aqua', which comes from the Latin word for 'water', joined with 'Maddas', which is a modification of the word 'Madda'.

'Madda' is modern Hebrew for 'Science'. I wished to pepper the Aqua Maddas cartoon with scientific facts and information about ocean animal species to capture the interest of curious minds.

However, when my mania and psychosis took hold, my cartoon character did not stay on paper or the computer. I became fully convinced that I *was* the aquatic being Aqua Maddas. I would speak for ages about this and would talk to anyone about my adventures as if they were genuine. I felt as though, through being this alter-ego, that spiritual force was talking to me. As Aqua Maddas, I 'visited' people and animals throughout history. I also thought I had seen the future and could predict the fate of the planet.

High doses of Olanzapine and Clonazepam alongside talk therapy helped me to become 'human' again. However, whilst being Aqua Maddas, I was able to work through some challenging emotions alongside telling others of my 'adventures'. My psychosis, in some ways, helped me to come to terms with the past trauma I had experienced. Although I know that I still need to work on myself, and will suffer from bipolar probably for the rest of my life, being Aqua Maddas helped me to deal with the reality of the abuse I suffered as a Small child.

I was fortunate in that I did not stay in the hospital for too long. I know that many people can stay there for months, even years and some people may never recover. However, I did have to spend a good couple of months at the Acute

Day Treatment Unit, or ADTU, following my hospitalisation.

Although I was mostly sane when discharged from the mental health hospital, I was still 'visited' by my alter-ego. I also needed time to recover from the experience of being in the hospital itself. At this point, I must stress that being in a mental hospital ward and surrounded by a lot of people all dealing with their demons, is a terrifying experience. You will be placed in the company of some severely dangerous people while you are at your most vulnerable.

Moving on, whilst I spent time at the ADTU, I retreated into myself and pushed many people away from me. Convinced that I was a liability to everyone I knew and loved, I isolated myself. All I would do is read books and tell people to leave me alone. This behaviour put a lot of strain on my relationship with Selene. I am sure it is no secret that it is incredibly tough to be romantically involved with someone suffering from bipolar mania and psychosis.

In fact, after the ordeal, our romantic relationship ended. However, because we went through so much together, Selene and I are still best friends to this day, and I am glad we continue to support each other. Selene stood by me through much of my recovery, and I will never forget that.

Recovering from psychosis can often feel like a lonely road. However, at the ADTU, I was able to connect with a few people who had similar experiences. It does seem to be the case that many Service Users have a history of childhood abuse, and it was a relief to find kindred spirits. I am also thankful for my friendship with Viktor. He helped me a lot during my time in the hospital ward.

Although I would not repeat the experience ever again, I am fortunate in some ways. The mental breakdown saved my life and helped me to heal from my PTSD. I am also grateful that I live in a time where there are treatments for severe mental health conditions and that people do not assume that I am suffering from something supernatural. Not so long ago, people with psychosis would be accused of being witches. Can you imagine that?

However, even now, I still have nightmares every night about slipping back into psychosis and becoming trapped again in the mental health hospital. I worry so much that I will never recover from bipolar and that I will have psychosis whilst doing something that could put others in danger, like driving. I agonise about how my mental health affects my friends, family, and anyone else close to me.

The shame from scaring everyone I know and love with my psychosis behaviours put me in a dark place for a long time. I will be frank; there were many times I felt like I should remove myself from the planet. Plus, the medication I have taken, including Olanzapine and Quetiapine, can worsen or even cause suicidal thoughts. If you know someone who has just been discharged from a mental health hospital, be extremely gentle with them. They are often engaged in a severe battle with their own minds.

As if that was not enough, those same medications result in an insatiable appetite for sweet food and often lead to a rapid increase in weight. It means that observing my Yom Kippur fast is even more difficult, but as well as that, there are obesity-associated health problems to watch out for as well as everything else. Again, be gentle with anyone you know who is taking anti-psychotic medication. Making fun of their weight gain is never acceptable.

But luckily for me, my PATH team is there for when my post-psychosis anxiety gets me down. Like PATH, I also hope that I can help people going through similar experiences. Sharing my story is the first step in this journey, and by helping others, I hope I can truly heal.

Now, I am rebuilding my life. I am still in work, and I have been fortunate with this. The drug discovery organisation that I work for has been very supportive and understanding. I hope that by raising awareness about psychosis, I can encourage more workplaces to be sensitive about similar mental health conditions.

I still swim, dive, and snorkel. With my action camera, I take photos of aquatic life and then use these as inspiration for my art. These activities are immensely therapeutic and grounding, especially in times of anxiety. I am still involved in efforts to protect the ocean. However, instead of threatening people to save the planet, I try to be a positive influencer on social media. I film myself removing plastic from the ocean, for example. Importantly, I do this as

Max, and not as my alter-ego, Aqua Maddas, despite my blog still harbouring that name.

So, for those in recovery, you are certainly not alone. Perhaps you are still in shock after having experienced psychosis or hearing voices? Maybe one day you will be able to see your psychosis as a blessing in disguise, but I do not want to promise that you will. I was able to heal from some of my past trauma whilst being 'Aqua Maddas'.

Furthermore, perhaps there is an evolutionary reason for psychosis? Maybe it is a process by which humanity can come to terms with awful circumstances beyond their control? Society can often point at us and think of us as 'monsters', especially if you, yourself, are convinced that you are some kind of sea monster! However, the real monster will always be the circumstances that push you over the edge. The mind will adapt, and be whatever it needs to be, to survive whatever Cursed Island describes your traumas."

A sea of faces appeared on Max's laptop screen and cheered in response to their speech. Max sighed happily, relieved that their time to speak in front of people was over, but also proud of themselves for opening up. They had even held back some tears, although it was evident that they were brimming with mixed emotions.

After a day of listening to the experiences of other Service Users and becoming dehydrated after crying so much, Max decided to spend some time outside.

Although they did not eat until much later that evening, they were happy to watch others eat. Specifically, they had taken some bird food to the nearby park and fed the ducks, geese, and moorhens. Whilst relishing the sounds of happy quacks, squeaks and honks from the hungry birds, Max felt the cool air on their skin and gazed at a beautiful pink sunset and sighed with relief.

"Every day, I am grateful for my freedom," Max muttered to themselves with a vibrant smile.

Another Swim

A month after the virtual Recovery Conference, Max and their new partner Robbie had treated themselves to a beach holiday in Cornwall over one long weekend. They sat on the soft sand of Holywell beach and enjoyed the magnificent surroundings, the gentle breeze, and the calm of the ocean lapping at the shore. Max combed the sand with their fingers and savoured the moment as cheeky seagulls scavenged leftover food from other beachgoers.

"Such a beautiful ocean," Max murmured to Robbie. "If there is a supreme being, I am grateful to them for giving me back my sanity so that I can sit freely here, enjoying such a wonderful beach. Plus, I do appreciate that my human hands and feet do not have claws. Although, sometimes, I do wish I had webs."

"You know, whenever you talk about your psychosis experience, I always wonder. Perhaps it was not bipolar mania? Perhaps some kind of alien did communicate with you, or take hold of your mind, to send a message to humanity?"

debated Robbie, their brown eyes wide from imaginative thinking.

"Haha, I love your theories," Max chuckled, poking Robbie's arm. "It's certainly refreshing to feel like I'm the sane one for a change."

"Are we going for a swim then?" Robbie asked, excitedly grabbing a snorkelling mask.

"I'm not sure yet. As you know, I do have a complicated relationship with the sea," Max muttered awkwardly. "I'm not sure what I should do."

"I know what you should do," smiled the scaly, spiky, blue-green creature that appeared beside Max. "There's always time for another swim."

Madness

What does it mean to be mad?
Do you wake up and decide,
Let's live differently today?
Instead of being productive,
Can we let our mind play?
Rather than being made to listen,
I think it is time to say;

Maybe our purpose in this world is more than
what we are told?
Are we here to produce, to earn, to reproduce,
to learn?
Or are we vessels of this universe, experiencing
itself first?
Or do our lives only serve to pay the mental
health Nurse?

Are we floating in an ocean of beautiful
dreams?
Is the air feeling particularly electric right now?
And I can feel what you are thinking, it seems.
I believe I can dance forever, but I don't even
know how.

And I seem to have a lot to shout about.
What do you mean by 'what?' and 'wow'?
And why are you calling an ambulance now?

What does it mean to be sane?
Does it mean pills forever?
Is it silencing every thought?
Trying not to think too much
And fearing being caught?
Is it control over our emotions?
Is logical thinking sought?

So, watch out who you call crazy - is anyone
really sane?
Do we honestly have an idea of the perfect,
model brain?
People can tell you what to do and how to
think,
You may be prescribed an unqualified shrink,
You may think that psychosis is bad, is a
character flaw,
But I say pack your things and float out of my
door.
Neurodiversity is what is real, and it is here to
stay.
So please, doctor, do not take all my madness
away...